3 –

THE CASE OF THE DISAPPEARING NEIGHBOR

"You were working for her!" Phyllis guessed.

Jane wasn't going to lie. "A little bit. For a couple of days before she disappeared."

"Was she afraid it was going to happen?" Helen asked.

"Not specifically. I would have directed her to the police if that had been the case. Of course, now I wish I had."

"Four spades." Helen ended the bidding and looked directly at Jane. "I know you won't talk about the specifics of a case, but you owe Phyllis and me this. Are we safe in our own homes? We both live in sight of Megan's house and Phyllis lives alone."

"I think so," Jane answered. "I didn't see Megan's disappearance coming, so I hesitate to say one hundred percent. But I believe what happened to Megan, whatever it was, was specific to Megan."

"Meaning?" Phyllis pressed.

"Either Megan was targeted, which seems most likely, or Megan took herself off, which seems less likely every day, but we can't dismiss it entirely. It's the better scenario for Megan so I can't quite give it up. . . ."

Books by Barbara Ross

Maine Clambake Mysteries
CLAMMED UP
BOILED OVER
MUSSELED OUT
FOGGED INN
ICED UNDER
STOWED AWAY
STEAMED OPEN
SEALED OFF

EGG NOG MURDER
(with Leslie Meier and Lee Hollis)
YULE LOG MURDER
(with Leslie Meier and Lee Hollis)
HAUNTED HOUSE MURDER
(with Leslie Meier and Lee Hollis)

Jane Darrowfield Mysteries
JANE DARROWFIELD, PROFESSIONAL
BUSYBODY
JANE DARROWFIELD AND THE MADWOMAN
NEXT DOOR

Published by Kensington Publishing Corp.

JANE DARROWFIELD AND THE MADWOMAN NEXT DOOR

Barbara Ross

KENSINGTON BOOKS
www.kensingtonbooks.com

KENSINGTON BOOKS are published by

Kensington Publishing Corp.
119 West 40th Street
New York, NY 10018

All Kensington titles, imprints, and distributed lines are available at special quantity discounts for bulk purchases for sales promotion, premiums, fund-raising, and educational or institutional use.

Special book excerpts or customized printings can also be created to fit specific needs. For details, write or phone the office of the Kensington Sales Manager: Kensington Publishing Corp., 119 West 40th Street, New York, NY 10018. Attn. Sales Department. Phone: 1-800-221-2647.

Kensington and the K logo Reg. U.S. Pat. & TM Off.

First Kensington Books Mass Market Paperback Printing: November 2020

ISBN-13: 978-1-4967-3075-6
ISBN-10: 1-4967-3075-5

10 9 8 7 6 5 4 3 2 1

Printed in the United States of America

This book is dedicated to my favorite brother, Rip Ross

Chapter One

The discreet sign at the end of her garden walk read JANE DARROWFIELD, PROFESSIONAL BUSYBODY. OFFICE HOURS M-W-F 8:00 A.M. TO NOON. NO JOB TOO SMALL. Nonetheless, Jane was surprised to see a familiar young woman moving down the flagstone walk along the side of her house clearly headed for her office door.

Jane was in her garden, hand watering her shrubs using a metal watering can. August in Massachusetts had been hot and sunny with hardly a cloud in the sky. Perfect weather for those vacationing at the beach on Cape Cod or in the Berkshires. But when the same weather rolled along, unbroken, into the middle of September, it had officially become a drought with attendant water restrictions. The little patch of lawn in Jane's West Cambridge yard had long since turned brown, but she was determined to keep her plants alive, watering them every other day as the rules allowed.

The woman raised her fist to knock on the glass door to the converted sunporch that served as Jane's office.

"I'm here!" Jane straightened up with an involuntary groan. "I'll be right along."

The young woman turned and smiled. Jane approached her, holding out her hand. "Jane Darrowfield."

The woman took the hand and shook, a firm, professional grasp. "Megan Larsen. I live next door."

"Of course." Jane and her neighbor had enjoyed a smiling and waving relationship for the ten months Megan had lived in the house. "Pleased to officially meet." Jane ushered Megan inside. "Coffee? Tea?"

"This isn't a social call." Megan flushed prettily. "Though I should have come by long before now. I have to run off to work in a moment. I'm a lawyer downtown."

Jane knew this, the neighborhood grapevine being what it was. There had been a lot of curiosity about the thirty-something single woman who had bought the house that was still among Jane's set called "the Baxter place," though the Baxters had been gone for more than two years. Jane also knew that by "downtown," Megan meant Boston, not Cambridge. Cambridge had many busy squares but no actual downtown.

Jane assessed her neighbor from close up. Her impressions from across the waist-high hedge that divided their front yards were confirmed. Megan Larsen was a very pretty woman. A luxurious mane of brown hair fell in gentle waves to below her shoulders. Her skin was clear, her eyes gray, and her figure trim and healthy looking. But her most arresting feature was her mouth. It was disproportionately large under her slightly upturned nose, and when she smiled, as she did tentatively now, her teeth were big and bright white with an ever-so-slight overbite. Her features weren't classic, but she was beautiful.

Megan was so tall she made Jane feel short, though she considered herself to be of normal height. Short and old, with hair that had to be helped to remain its original honey-blond color. Megan Larsen wore a beautifully tailored, sleeveless green dress. Jane was in her gardening clothes—shorts and an old polo shirt.

She gestured toward one of the chairs across from her desk, and her guest sat. Jane sat too, pulling her rolling chair forward until her shorts were hidden by the desk. They were silent for a moment.

"What can I do for you, Ms. Larsen?" It was apparent the young woman was having trouble starting the conversation.

"Call me Megan, please." The woman paused, then took a deep gulp of air and the words rushed out. "I want you to figure out if I'm crazy."

Chapter Two

Jane didn't try to hide her surprise, though she consciously softened her features with a pleasant smile before she spoke. "I'm afraid I'm not that kind of professional. My practice involves fixing small problems that require discreet handling. Things that, while vexing, aren't appropriate for the police. I have no therapeutic credentials whatsoever. I'd be happy to give you some names."

Megan nodded, flashing her big smile. "You are exactly what I need. Someone discreet who can observe my life and tell me if my symptoms are, as I believe, caused by something real or if they're in my head."

In spite of her better instincts, Jane was intrigued. She opened the small red leather-bound notebook that sat on her desktop and picked up a pen. "And your symptoms are?"

"Flashing lights wake me in the middle of the night,

but when I open my eyes, the room is dark and I'm in a pool of sweat."

"It's been quite warm."

"I have central air."

"There may be medical reasons," Jane offered.

Megan held up a cautioning palm. "I've been to my primary care physician, and she's even referred me to an endocrinologist. There's no physical cause, if that's what you mean."

It had been what Jane had meant. She motioned for Megan to go on.

But Megan did not.

Finally Jane said, "Unless you want to hire me to watch you sleep, I don't see what I can do."

Megan's brow creased and her full lips pursed. They sat like that for another few moments. "That's not the worst of it." She hesitated again. "I've been forgetting things. And losing time. Having blackouts, I suppose you would say." The rest came out in a rush. "And hearing voices. I believe someone is stalking me."

Jane's pulse rate increased steadily through the recitation. The woman sitting in front of her looked sane, but a long life had taught Jane not all lunatics looked as if they'd recently escaped from Bedlam. "This seems quite serious. You must see a psychiatrist or psychologist as soon as possible."

Megan inhaled deeply and then let out a long breath. "I don't want to do that. Not yet, anyway. I'm up for partner at my law firm this fall, and I don't want either the HR department or my insurance company to know about this." She tapped a finger on Jane's big mahogany desk. "Especially if my symptoms aren't caused by mental illness. Because I don't think they are. I believe someone really is out to get me."

Jane didn't point out that this was exactly what someone would believe if they were suffering from a major mental illness. Instead she said, "Will you promise me that if I determine there are no tangible reasons for your symptoms, you will consult a qualified psychologist or psychiatrist?"

Megan held her hand up, oath-taking style. "I promise."

"I charge by the hour or by the day." Jane named a healthy figure.

"Does that mean you'll take my case?"

Jane closed the notebook. "Yes. When would you like to get started?"

"As soon as possible." Megan stood. "Can you meet me at my house this evening? I'll leave work early. Around six o'clock?"

Jane agreed and walked Megan to the door. They said their good-byes, and Jane watched her neighbor's retreating back as she made her way down the flagstones to the sidewalk.

Chapter Three

"What do we think of the young woman who moved in next door to me?" Jane was at her weekly bridge game with Helen Graham, Phyllis Goldstein, and Irma Brittleson, her great and good friends. They were at Phyllis's house today, across the street from Helen's and around the corner from Jane's.

"In the Baxter place," Helen said. The Baxters had been middle-aged when Jane had moved into the neighborhood as a young faculty wife. Their teenagers had babysat for her son, Jonathan. A couple of years ago they'd grown too old for the stairs and the snow and the gutters. They sold up and moved to a senior living community. That's when the flipper bought it.

"I only know her to wave hello," Helen said. "She seems nice enough." Helen was their golden goddess—slim, athletic, her white hair worn in the same pageboy she'd sported since her twenties.

"She recycles, keeps her yard neat, and has someone shovel her walk," Phyllis added. "Nothing to complain about. Though I had hoped for a family with children." Phyllis was small and pleasantly round. Her deep, raspy voice marked her as a smoker or a drinker, though she was neither.

Jane, Helen, and Phyllis sighed the same regretful sigh. There was always the hope of young families moving into the neighborhood, mirrors of their own when they'd moved in as young wives. The big houses were perfect for families. The curving streets, dead-ends, and cul-de-sacs were made for Hot Wheels races, street hockey games, and parents standing out on a summer evening visiting and gossiping, perhaps with a cold beverage.

But there hadn't been a new young family for years. The neighborhood, a little island on the far western edge of Cambridge, tucked between Brattle Street, Huron Avenue, and Fresh Pond Parkway, was lovely. Forty years before, it had been affordable for the single-income family of a not-yet-tenured Harvard professor, as Jane's ex-husband, Francis, had been; a not-quite-a-doctor resident as Helen's husband had been; and a not-yet-a-business-owner engineer as Phyllis's late husband was at the time. But that had changed over the years as the houses had become ever more expensive. In the last decade the values had accelerated at warp speed.

"To be honest, I was pleased she wasn't an investor." Helen dealt the hand with a practiced efficiency. "And that she actually lives there. When I saw it was being flipped, the way it was renovated, I assumed it would be the usual."

"The usual?" Irma studied her hand. She hadn't taken part in the conversation to that point. She was the new member of the group, having been a player for only twenty-nine of the bridge game's thirty-eight years. She had a thin face and a beaked nose, and she wore her lovely steel-gray hair in an elaborate bun. She lived with her ancient mother in an apartment in a big two-family house a mile and a half away, a half a dozen distinct neighborhoods from the others' homes in their dense little city.

"Chinese billionaires, Russian oligarchs, Middle Eastern royalty, Eurotrash." Phyllis rearranged her cards. "Moving money out of their countries for whatever reason."

"Parking it all over the world," Jane added. "And lately, here."

"And they don't live here. That's what gets me," Helen said. "Sometimes they have kids in local colleges or boarding schools, and they have wild parties and trash the houses over their breaks, but mostly the windows are dark."

Not that they wouldn't have been anyway, Jane thought. Investors loved the brick, stone, or stucco homes in the neighborhood, with their generous 1920s proportions, but they couldn't leave well enough alone. As the houses had turned over, additions had taken up even more of their tiny lots, and giant open-plan kitchens with family rooms had grown out of the backs or sides of the houses. The formal front living rooms were dwarfed by the "great rooms" and seldom used.

"When I saw how the guy who flipped that house did it up, I assumed he was looking for foreign investors too," Helen said.

Since the boom, perusing real estate websites had become an obsession in the neighborhood, and home prices were the most common topic of conversation. Jane had even attended the open house when Megan's place had been on the market. After all, it was right next door.

"But Megan Larsen . . ." Jane prompted. She couldn't tell them why she was asking, but she would try one more time.

"Perfectly nice, but not what I expected," Phyllis said.

"Or hoped," Helen amended. "I dealt and pass."

"Pass," Jane said.

"Pass," Irma said.

"Or hoped," Phyllis agreed. "Three no trump."

"Phyllis!" The other three yelled in unison, a practiced chorus.

"I told you I didn't have enough points for an opening bid," Jane protested.

"We shall see." Phyllis was an aggressive bidder. Sometimes she even made it.

Chapter Four

At six o'clock that evening, Jane was on her front stoop when Megan walked down their winding street, lugging a briefcase that looked far too heavy for her.

Megan waved from the end of Jane's walk. "Hello! Come on over." Jane met her and walked with her past the hedge and down her driveway.

Megan's big brick house sat slightly farther back on its lot than Jane's house did, which was nice for both of them, affording more privacy and sunlight than might otherwise have been the case since the houses were only a driveway-width apart.

Unlike most houses in the neighborhood, Megan's had an attached garage. During the renovation the developer had torn down the free-standing one-car garage and rebuilt it with two bays, permissible because the structure extended no farther than the original toward the property line. Jane knew from the open house that the area above the garage was now a luxurious master suite.

Megan put the briefcase down in the drive and fiddled with a keypad beside the garage door. The double door rolled up with a *clackety-clackety-clack*. Jane was surprised to see the garage was empty, though when she thought about it, she'd never seen Megan in a car. Jane had heard that young people often didn't own cars these days, relying instead on bicycles, public transportation, rideshares, and rentals. Indeed, there was a sturdy red bicycle leaning against the back wall of the garage.

Megan entered more numbers on the keypad on the door from the garage to the house while a camera stood sentry over the door. Once they'd climbed the two-step riser and were inside the house, Megan punched more numbers into the security system to disarm it.

Jane watched with interest. It wasn't uncommon for people to have alarm systems in her increasingly tony neighborhood, particularly in houses such as Megan's that had been gut renovated. But in Jane's experience the systems were generally activated only when residents were away for an extended time, not for a simple day at work. Break-ins were not unknown. There had been a rash of them more than a decade ago. But they were exceedingly rare.

Megan's house was lovely. When Jane had come through during the open house, her first impression had been one of light and brightness. Most of the downstairs walls had been removed during the renovation.

She and Megan entered into an open kitchen with tall ceilings, white-white cabinets, a big kitchen island, and white countertops. The kitchen extended to the front of the house. A comfy-looking white leather couch, a coffee table, bookshelves, and a TV mounted on the outside wall filled the remaining space.

Jane was shocked to realize that the furniture was the same as it had been the last time she'd been there. Apparently, Megan had bought not only the house but also the furniture it had been staged with. She had bought, fully, the vision of the life the developer had been selling.

On the other hand, the house wasn't obsessively neat. There were personal touches—a crocheted afghan askew on the back of the white leather couch and bowls for a pet of some kind on the kitchen floor. Expensive brass cooking pans hung from a rack over the kitchen island. An antique painting of a lamb was over the fireplace, which should have looked out of place in the sleek room but somehow fit right in. Jane found the hominess and slight mess reassuring. In her experience, people who viewed their homes as stage sets—places where the perfect setting would result in a perfect life—often had problems. Megan truly lived in her house.

A half-full glass mug of light brown liquid sat on the coffee table. Megan whisked it away, stowing it in the big farmer's sink as she offered Jane a drink. "Wine? Iced tea? Water?"

Jane accepted the wine. Megan's most alarming symptoms—the lost time, voices, blackouts, the paranoia—could be related to alcohol consumption. It would be interesting to watch her drink.

Megan pulled an open bottle of white wine out of the fridge, grabbed two fancy crystal wineglasses, and led Jane outdoors to a bistro set on a small flagstone patio. The day had cooled down enough to make the outdoors pleasant.

The yard was smaller than Jane's because of the way

the house sat on its lot. The tiny bit of grass was mowed, and despite the drought, the shrubs that the developer had added were thriving. Megan, or someone, must be caring for them. A high stockade fence separated Megan's backyard from Jane's. Jane could look down onto a sliver of the yard from the bedroom at the back of her house, the bedroom Jane still thought of, despite more than a decade of disuse, as her son Jonathan's room. But Jane never went in there if she could avoid it, so until that moment she couldn't have reported on the state of Megan's back garden.

Megan poured the wine. Jane waited to see if her neighbor would ease the way into the conversation. When she did not, Jane broached the reason they were both there. "When did you begin to feel—"

Megan smiled. "Like I was losing it?" Megan wiggled her bottom on the cast-iron chair, settling in. "I can't say exactly. It's been a gradual thing. Six months, maybe?"

Jane counted backward in her head. Six months would have been March. Megan had moved in during November. "Did the symptoms start all at once?"

"No. The first thing was the night sweats. Then the flashing lights. The rest came after."

"These lights flash when your eyes are closed?" Jane clarified.

"Yes. They wake me in the night. But when I open my eyes, they're gone. By then I'm fully awake, my heart is pounding, and I can't get back to sleep."

"What about the voices?"

"The same thing. I hear someone talking downstairs. I wake up and I'm awake."

"You hear the voices only when you're asleep?"

"And then I wake up," Megan confirmed.

"Is it possible you're dreaming?"

"I'd hoped that was true for a long time. But how can you explain that I wake up bathed in sweat? I didn't dream that."

"Are you getting enough rest?"

"I'm certain I'm not. I have a stressful job and work long hours. Being up for a couple of hours at night isn't helping."

"Let's talk about the other symptoms," Jane said. "Start with losing time."

Megan shifted in her seat again. But this time it wasn't the movement of a woman getting comfortable. It was the drawing back and into herself of a person distinctly uncomfortable. "When I wake up in the night like that, I try to get back to sleep, but I usually can't. I go downstairs and read or watch a little TV. I try to relax and not obsess about the time and not sleeping, because that only makes it harder to get back to sleep. But then I look up and hours have gone by. Time I don't remember. Time that isn't measured by pages read or TV movies watched. I can't account for it."

Jane focused on keeping her face neutral, interested. Not alarmed or surprised. "Is it possible you're dozing off?" Jane had reached an age where dozing off on the couch late at night was a distinct possibility. Or any time, really.

Megan shook her head. "I don't think so. If I was asleep, wouldn't I be conscious of waking?"

Would she be? Jane tried to think if she was conscious of waking every day. "And when this time has passed, what do you do?" she asked gently.

"I go back to bed and sleep until my alarm goes off." Megan paused. "Early. Way too early. I'm always exhausted."

Could sleeplessness alone account for Megan's symptoms? Jane wasn't sure. "Is this every night?"

"No, not quite every night, but almost. I'm always relieved when I have a night when I sleep through."

"Did you speak to your doctor about your sleep problems?"

"I did. She prescribed something. I haven't picked it up at the pharmacy yet. I'm wary of taking it. The medication comes with a lot of side effects. I need to be sharp at work. I can't be walking around like a zombie."

Jane let that go. Surely losing several hours of sleep almost every night wasn't helping her mental acuity either. "And the forgetting things?"

"I'll be certain I had put the security alarm on when I went up to bed, but I'll check my phone before I go to sleep and the system isn't activated. Or I'll be sure I closed the garage door, but when I come downstairs on these wakeful nights, it will be wide open."

"That kind of memory lapse sounds pretty normal to me."

"It's not like me."

Jane tried to think if she had ever noticed Megan's garage door open during the day. It was the kind of thing, if it happened frequently, that would have been remarked on in the neighborhood. She decided she had not.

"I noticed the bowls beside the kitchen island," Jane said. "You have a pet."

"Wembly, a marmalade cat," Megan confirmed. "He's around inside somewhere. He's a big guy, but shy. He doesn't like it when I have other people in the house.

Luckily for him, I rarely do. I'm not home enough to do much entertaining."

Jane wished Wembly had been a dog, more sensitive to intruders, more communicative about changes in the environment. "How does Wembly react when these things occur, like the voices?"

Megan shrugged. "He likes it when I'm up during the night. He loves to sit with me on the couch."

"The feeling you're being stalked or followed, when did that start?" Jane prompted.

"More recently. Maybe three or four months ago." Megan looked at the tabletop. Her long brown hair hung down on either side of her face.

"Have you noticed someone lurking outside or following as you walk?"

Megan smiled and made a noise that was almost a laugh, perhaps at herself. "No, nothing like that. No faces peering in the windows. It's more a feeling of being watched that makes the hair on the back of my neck stand up."

Jane thought losing several hours of sleep multiple nights in a row might explain Megan's paranoia. On the other hand . . . "Let's try this," she said. "If someone were stalking you, who would it be?"

"I can't imagine."

"You're a lawyer. A disgruntled client perhaps?" Jane suggested.

Megan actually did laugh this time, a big full-throated guffaw. "I'm a real estate lawyer, not a criminal lawyer or even in civil litigation. My clients do sometimes act as if their transactions are life-and-death matters, but believe me, they're not. It's land deals, building sales and purchases, zoning, planning, and historical commission approvals."

"And none of these life-or-death matters have resulted in interactions with anyone you'd suspect?"

"No." Megan shook her head. "I'm sure of it."

"How about other people in your life? There was a young man who helped you move in. I noticed him carrying boxes from your truck."

That Megan had bought all the staging furniture in the house explained the smallish rental truck she'd turned up with on that cool gray day early in November. There'd been a lot of speculation about the new owner around the neighborhood. Jane had watched the handsome man and pretty woman in their midthirties carry boxes into the house. She'd assumed they were a couple and had been mildly baffled when he'd disappeared from the scene.

"That was Ben. My ex. We were together for twelve years starting in law school and lived together for the last five until I moved here. But it didn't work out. He wasn't ready to make more of a commitment to a shared life, and I was unwilling to wait. This house"—Megan gestured through the patio doors to the inside—"is my statement that I'm unwilling to wait to get the life I want. Certainly, I'm unwilling to wait for a man."

Megan's statement did explain the four-bedroom house on a quiet street. The house was aspirational, a statement about the life Megan planned.

"Exes have been known to stalk," Jane ventured.

Megan didn't hesitate. "Not Ben. He's the most laid-back, practical guy you'll ever meet. We parted friends. We wanted different things. But it wasn't ugly. That's why he helped me move."

"And there's no one else? No one you can think of who might want to pursue you or hurt you?"

Megan's brow furrowed. Double lines too deep for someone her age appeared over the upturned nose. "Well, maybe one." She paused, taking her time, gathering her words. Then she blew air out in one quick puff and continued. "A few months ago, I went on an online date. Ben and I were broken up, and I was feeling the need to get back out there."

"Online dating can work very well," Jane said. "That's how I met my . . ." She hesitated. *Boyfriend* was such a ridiculous word at her age. "Person," she finished. Though both she and Harry had thought they were meeting someone else at the time.

"Then you had better luck than I did," Megan said. "I met this guy for coffee at Peet's in Harvard Square. Just coffee. I wasn't impressed, but I guess he was, because he was really aggressive, pressing me to go on a real date, a weekend away, a honeymoon." Megan picked up her wineglass and drank. It was the first sip she'd taken since they'd sat down. "That last is an exaggeration, but barely. I couldn't get out of there fast enough."

"How long ago was this?"

Megan cast her gray eyes heavenward and squinched up her pert nose, trying to remember. "January. It was a New Year's resolution to get out there more. The resolution lasted for exactly one date." She pulled her phone out of the pocket of her dress and scrolled through her calendar. "Here it is. January twelfth."

"Have you heard from him since?"

"He contacted me through the dating app a couple of times. I didn't respond." Despite the warm fall evening, Megan wrapped her arms around herself and shuddered. "He was awful."

"And what was his name?" Jane asked.

"Howard. Howard Berg. *Borg*." She shuddered again. "Ugh."

Jane took the red notebook out of her handbag and wrote down the name, getting Megan to spell it for her. It seemed as good a place to start as any. "There's something else I need from you," she said. "Have you told anyone besides me about your concerns?"

"Absolutely not. I don't want people to think I'm crazy. That's why I came to you for help. I want someone who hasn't been part of my life."

"Good," Jane replied. "I need the name of a friend, a very good friend you trust completely. Someone who's known you for a long time and who will give me an honest assessment of you and whether you've changed over the past several months."

"Is that really necessary?"

"Yes," Jane answered. "Who better to assess us than our friends."

"What will you tell this person about why you're talking to them?"

"I'll tell them whatever you would like, within limits. You're going to call to say I'll be setting up a meeting, so you can give the reason."

Megan thought for another few moments, the crease in her brow appearing again. "Talk to my friend Andy Bromfield. We went to law school together and we've shared an office at our law firm for seven years. No one has seen me through more ups and downs. I'll call him and tell him who you are and why you want to talk to him. I'll figure out what to tell him."

Jane had finished her wine, but Megan had only had the one sip. Megan grabbed her nearly full glass and led them inside, where they left the glasses on the countertop by the sink. Behind them was a desk built into the kitchen cabinetry, with a fancy, covered bulletin board at eye level for someone seated and a blackboard above that.

"What's your cell number?" Megan asked.

Jane rattled off the familiar numbers. Megan wrote Jane's full name and cell number on the blackboard in a large flowing script. A poster tacked on the wall next to the bulletin board was covered with photos and words cut from magazines. "Visualize success!" the poster proclaimed. There were photos of adorable babies, tropical islands, cats, and kittens.

"What's your number?" Jane asked.

Megan took a business card from a receptacle on the desk, scribbled on it, and handed it to Jane. MEGAN LARSEN, ATTORNEY-AT-LAW. BOOKERMAN, DIGBY, AND EADE. Under her name was an address, a landline number and extension, a cell number, and an e-mail address. In her flowing handwriting, Megan had added Andy Bromfield's name and cell number.

Jane thanked her, and Megan let her out through the garage. Jane waved from the sidewalk as Megan lowered the door, *clackety-clackety-clack*.

Chapter Five

The next morning Jane met Andy Bromfield at a coffee shop around the corner from a handsome tower in the Boston financial district where Bookerman, Digby, and Eade's offices were spread across seven floors.

Jane had heard of the firm. There weren't many law firms of that size in Boston. But the name was about all she knew. Her former employment at a major telecommunications company had taught her a lot about finance, technology, and people, but she'd never had much to do with lawyers. As a matter of fact, in her various roles as she rose through the ranks in management, it would have been a bad sign indeed if she'd had a lot of contact with lawyers.

She'd read Megan's bio and Andy's, along with those of other members of the real estate department, on the firm's website. Bookerman, Digby, and Eade employed hundreds of lawyers focused on specialties including corporate, environmental, health care, and litigation. There were satellite offices in New York; Washington, DC; and Paris. Jane was impressed and exhausted by the scope of it by the time she'd stopped reading.

Andy Bromfield was in his midthirties like Megan, a lanky man with curly brown hair that framed a lengthening forehead and large protuberant ears. He wore glasses with black frames; a plaid, short-sleeved shirt; and khakis. Jane still found it a little odd when lawyers, bankers, and business executives didn't wear suits to work, but she'd retired recently enough to be familiar with the phenomenon. He'd get dressed up only for court, she imagined, and maybe important client meetings. He hadn't expected to see anyone important that day.

Andy hustled them to a corner booth, clearly understanding that their conversation was to be confidential. "How can I help you, Mrs. Darrowfield?" he asked once they were seated.

"Jane, please."

"Andy." He reached across the table and shook her hand.

"Andy, I know Megan contacted you about this conversation." The waitress arrived and took their order, a cup of coffee for each of them, Jane's with cream and his black.

"She did, though I'm not sure I understand." Andy's smile was wary.

"Megan's been experiencing some issues lately that concern her. She hasn't had any luck with her medical doctor, so she's asked me to look into them."

"She's asked you because—I'm sorry. Why has she asked you, in particular?"

"Because I'm her neighbor. I live next door." Jane said

it definitively, as if her answer was the most logical in the world.

Andy frowned. He wasn't entirely buying it, but Megan had asked him. Jane watched the push and pull play across his long face. Finally, he said, "Shoot. Ask me anything."

"You and Megan have been friends for a long time?"

"Since elementary school. We went to the same schools growing up, then Harvard undergrad and law school."

Jane hadn't realized they'd known each other that long. Megan hadn't mentioned anything prior to law school.

The waitress delivered the coffee in bright white ceramic mugs. The coffee shop was an old-fashioned one, not the kind of place where people sat and worked on their laptops all day. It was quiet in the hours between breakfast and lunch, with just a few customers scattered at the long counter and in the booths.

As the waitress moved away, Andy resumed talking. "Megan and I have shared an office for seven years. You can't help but overhear each other's conversations. You can cope with the lack of privacy by confiding in each other or by putting up pretend walls. Megan and I have embraced our proximity."

Perfect. He'd known Megan for a long time and spent hours in her company every day. Jane charged ahead. "Have you noticed any change in Megan's behavior lately?"

Andy sat back in the booth, seriously considering the question. "What does lately mean?"

"The last several months."

Andy didn't hesitate. "Megan is as solid as a rock. It's one of the best things about her. Of course, there was some drama around her breakup with Ben. I felt badly for her because she was hurt and also because he forced her to be the one to pull the plug. But she's better off without him in my opinion."

Jane pondered. Was this an avenue to explore? "Why better off?"

Andy lifted the white coffee mug to his mouth and took a swallow. "Once they got together in law school, Megan was all-in with Ben. She really loved him. But Ben . . ." Andy put the mug down. "I always thought he loved the idea of Megan much more than he loved the living, breathing person."

"What does that mean?"

Andy clearly didn't want to bad-mouth Ben but did want to be honest. In the end, his loyalty to Megan won out. "I mean that Ben wants to think of himself as the type of guy who would have a beautiful, incredibly intelligent woman, who is as accomplished as he is, as his girlfriend or wife. But really, I don't think that's what Ben wants at all. He wants someone who'll cook his dinner and raise his kids and meet him at the door with a nice pinot noir at the end of a long day. He couldn't admit that to himself, but it kept him from fully committing to Megan. So she had to break it off. He gave her no choice."

"How do they get along now? Do they still see each other?"

"Boston is a big small town, so of course they run into each other. His firm played our firm in softball last month."

"How did he and Megan interact?"

"Fine. Like grown-ups." Andy paused. "What does all this have to do with what Megan's asked you?"

"Megan's become worried about her health and her safety over the last few months."

Andy had picked up the white mug again, but he put it down on the Formica table with a *thunk*. The color drained from his face. "And she thinks it has something to do with Ben?"

"No, no, no, no." The last thing Jane wanted was to trash Ben's reputation if there was no cause. Boston *was* a big small town.

"Is she sick?" Andy's voice rose, causing a few of the other customers to glance over toward their booth. "I noticed she's left the office for a few doctors' appointments recently."

"Nothing like that," Jane reassured him. "Would you say she's under a lot of stress?"

Andy brought his voice back down to a conversational level. "We both are, with this partnership thing coming up. We're evenly matched. Balanced strengths and weaknesses. If they were smart they'd take both of us, but there's only one slot."

"And yet you've remained good friends, even though you're competitors for the partnership. That must be tricky."

"It will be what it will be. One of us will win and one will lose, but we'll still be friends."

Jane nodded. "So no big changes in Megan's personality over the last few months?"

He shook his head. "Truly, no. I'm amazed you're even asking."

"Does Megan have any clients who are particularly unhappy with her, or maybe a little too interested?"

Andy chuckled. "She attracts a lot of attention. She's got it all—beauty, brains, charm to spare. But no. Her clients love her. That's one of the reasons she's such tough competition for me." He tapped the face of his high-tech watch, and it lit up with the time. "I don't know what to tell you. I'm not even sure I know what you want. Like I said, Megan is as solid as a rock. I'd put my life in her hands if it came down to it."

The waitress had left the bill on the table. Jane's hand moved toward it, but Andy snatched it up. "I insist," he said. "Feel free to call me if you have more questions. I have to run."

Jane thanked him and watched him walk out the door. She'd enjoy the cool of the coffee shop for a few more minutes. She had plenty of time to get back to Harvard Square to meet with Howard Borg.

Chapter Six

Howard Borg's unusual name made him easy for Jane to track down. He had his own small company, Lockdown Cybersecurity Limited, LLC, with an office in a co-working space in Kendall Square. The description of what his company did was vague and confusingly tech. There was a photo of him on the website with the title of principal.

Jane took the Red Line to meet him at Peet's in Harvard Square. She'd been surprised when he suggested the location. He'd have to take the subway or bike to get there. Why didn't he want to meet her closer to his office?

Jane was well known at Peet's. She and Harry had met there fourteen months before. One of the baristas, Tonya, had witnessed their first meeting and claimed credit for their pairing, though in truth she'd done nothing except cheer them on. She greeted them warmly whenever they came in. Today was no exception.

"Where's your better half?" Tonya asked when Jane ordered a cold water. She was awash in coffee.

"At his house. He'll come over to mine for dinner tonight."

"You tell him I said hello."

Jane found a table for two and sat facing the door. She recognized Borg from his photo the moment he entered. He looked around, evidently not seeing anyone he recognized, and ordered an Americano. He was sharp featured and thin, with long light brown hair hanging over his shirt collar.

"Over here, Mr. Borg," Jane called when he'd been served. She started to rise to greet him, but he'd sunk into the chair across from her before she could get up. He'd seemed annoyed by her call, and she was surprised he'd agreed to meet her. In the end, his curiosity must have gotten the best of him.

"You told me this was in regard to a personal matter," he said.

Jane could see that in a photo on a dating site he might appear to have potential, but in person he was off-putting. When he spoke, he leaned so far toward her, she involuntarily pushed her chair back. "Yes. I'm working for Megan Larsen."

"Who?" Howard pushed his skinny neck even farther in Jane's direction. She pushed her chair back once again.

"Megan Larsen. You met on a dating app last winter and had coffee right here."

He shook his shaggy head. "Sorry. Not ringing any bells."

Really? Megan wasn't forgettable. "Long brown hair, gray eyes, gorgeous complexion."

"That's a generic sort of description." Howard gulped his coffee. "I meet a lot of women."

"Lawyer, lives in Cambridge," Jane prompted.

"Lawyer, you say? That does ring a bell. I think I did meet her. Frankly, she didn't make much of an impression. Way too meek for my taste. I wasn't interested in moving forward. Like I said, I can barely remember her."

Actually, he'd said he didn't remember her at all, but Jane didn't contradict him.

"What's this about? Is she saying I did something to her? Because I absolutely didn't. We were together maybe ten minutes."

His memory was returning. "Nothing like that," Jane reassured him. "She needs to document her activities on that day. You can confirm you met Ms. Larsen here at eleven a.m. on Wednesday, January twelfth?"

"Does she need an alibi or something?" He pulled his lips back in a feral grin.

"Nothing like that. It's an insurance matter." Thinking about it on the way over, this was the best excuse Jane could come up with for such an out-of-the-blue conversation. Vague but official sounding.

Howard pulled his phone from his pocket and scrolled through something on the screen. "This past January?" he asked. When Jane nodded he said, "I met somebody here for coffee on January twelfth at eleven. To confirm it was her I'd have to see a photo."

Jane brought out her own phone and pulled up Megan's photo on her law firm's website.

Howard took the phone and held it to his face. "Yeah, coulda been her. Like I said, I don't remember. If you want me to swear to it for some kind of insurance thing, I'd have to see her again in person."

That was never going to happen. "Thank you for your time, Mr. Borg. You've been very helpful."

He picked up his coffee and left without saying another word, pausing by the door to get a lid for the paper cup.

Tonya appeared next to Jane's table. "I wouldn't have said you were his type."

Jane laughed. "It was nothing like that. A business meeting. Does he have a type?"

"He likes them tall, brunette, and way out of his league."

Just like Megan. "Does he meet a lot of women here?"

"Hundreds," Tonya said. "Seriously, he's here at least a couple of times a week."

"Do any of these coffee meetups ever work?" Jane asked. "Do the women ever agree to go out with him?"

"Never. And once they leave, he hangs around and hits on us." Tonya hugged herself and moved her tiny body in an exaggerated shudder. "Uck."

Jane understood what she meant. "Thanks, Tonya. You've been very helpful. Harry and I will be back soon."

"Have a good day, Jane. Try to stay cool out there."

Chapter Seven

Out on the sidewalk, Jane contemplated her next move. So far, everything had been as Megan had said it would be. Andy Bromfield was a good friend, even though he was a competitor for a plum partnership at their law firm. Howard Borg was a creepy guy. Jane couldn't imagine Megan going on a date with him, even though Howard claimed it was he who was disinterested.

But what about Ben Fox, the ex-boyfriend? When she'd checked out Megan's social media presence, Jane had found plenty of old photos posted by Megan of Ben and Megan together. Posed in front of a Christmas tree, on an island vacation, on the Esplanade at the Boston Pops Fourth of July celebration. But there'd been no photos of Ben for months, exactly as Megan had told it.

Andy had said that Ben's law firm played Bookerman, Digby, and Eade in softball. Presumably his was also a big Boston outfit. Using the browser on her smartphone, it didn't take long for Jane to find him. He worked at Ronson, Berriman, and Shoemaker at the business end of Beacon Street downtown. Jane walked back to the subway and headed inbound.

By the time Jane got to the office tower that housed Ronson, Berriman, and Shoemaker, she was drenched in perspiration from the short walk from Park Street. The air-conditioning in the lobby hit her like a punch. She shivered her way to the seventeenth floor.

The receptionist was young and uncertain. Jane sensed she might be a temp. She looked up Ben Fox's name on a sheet of paper taped to her desk and called him.

"There's a Jane Darrowfield here to see you."

She listened, then looked up at Jane. "What is this in regard to?"

"Megan Larsen."

The receptionist repeated what Jane had said and listened again. "He's finishing up a meeting. He can see you in a few minutes." She replaced the phone. "Would you like water or coffee?"

Jane refused both and asked directions to the restroom. By the time she returned to the lobby, Ben Fox was waiting for her.

He introduced himself, shook Jane's hand, and led her to his office. Unlike Andy and Megan, he had his own space. Perhaps because he didn't have an officemate, he'd allowed his work to expand to take up the entirety of the small room. There were piles of paper on his desk, the credenza, and the floor. He cleared a dozen file folders off a chair and offered Jane a seat.

"While you were in the reception area, I called Megan to ask why you were here."

"Obviously she confirmed it was okay to talk to me."

Ben walked around behind his desk and sat. "Obviously." He was good-looking and tall, with expensively cut brown hair and warm brown eyes. He had a firm chin and a finely chiseled nose. Like Andy Bromfield, he wore a crisp cotton plaid summer shirt and khakis. Unlike Andy Bromfield, Ben still had all his hair. He and Megan had made an extraordinarily good-looking couple.

"Did Megan explain what I'm after?" Jane asked.

"A little. But I have to say I don't understand it."

"When is the last time you saw Megan?"

Ben hesitated, as if trying to remember. "Four weeks ago. Her firm played mine in softball. We're each on our respective teams." He shrugged. "We're broken up, but we were together for twelve years. We're in the same profession and we have a lot of friends in common. We're inevitably going to see each other."

"How is it when you see each other?"

"It's fine. We're adults." *Exactly what Andy Bromfield had said.* Ben met her eyes, unblinking and apparently unwilling to expand.

Jane leaned forward in the office chair. "Since you broke up, have you noticed anything different about Megan?"

"Different how?"

"Have you noticed any changes in her personality or behavior? That sort of thing."

Ben frowned. "Megan hired *you* to tell *her* if *she* is behaving differently?" He was skeptical.

Jane was undeterred. "She told you it was okay to talk

to me, correct? Call her back if you want to know if this is okay."

Ben's hand wavered over the handset of his phone, but then he thought better of it. "You mean other than the fact that she's not with me?" he answered. "No. Same old Megan. She's dealt better with our breakup than I have, if you want to know the truth."

"Why did you break up, Mr. Fox?"

"Ben, please. I'm guessing Megan told you she left me because I couldn't commit and she wanted to get on with her life—buy a home, have children, stuff like that." He looked at Jane, who nodded slightly, and he went on. "That's exactly what happened. She couldn't take me diddling around anymore and gave me my walking papers."

Jane waited to see if he would say more. This time her patience was rewarded.

"I threw it all away. I don't know why I did, why I couldn't step up. I've been sorry every day since." His voice was heavy with regret.

"Have you tried to get back together with Megan? Perhaps gone by her place? Waited outside?"

Ben's brows rose. "What are you suggesting?" When Jane didn't respond, after a moment he said, "Anyway, the answer is no. I hung around for a while after Megan said we were done. I even helped her move out of our place into the house she bought. But she made it clear I'd had my chance. More than my chance." He paused again. "I don't blame her."

He didn't sound bitter, and to the extent he sounded angry, it was clearly anger directed at himself. Jane wondered why this man who had been with Megan for so long and clearly loved her hadn't, indeed, stepped up. Perhaps Andy Bromfield's theory about him was correct. He didn't want a wife like Megan.

"Is there anything about Megan, anything at all, that made you hesitate to marry her?" Jane asked.

Ben shook his head. "Nothing. The problem with our relationship is that I am an idiot."

Chapter Eight

Jane took the Red Line home, turning over what she had learned. All three men were exactly as Megan had described them. She wasn't deluded about her relationships, that was for sure. None of them had indicated that Megan was the slightest bit unbalanced. The more Jane got to know about her, the healthier she seemed.

But that didn't mean Megan's symptoms were imaginary. It probably meant the opposite. Something real was driving her experiences. If she wasn't mentally ill, what was it?

When Jane got home she went straight to her office. She needed to do research.

Her first thought was that there might be some environmental cause for Megan's symptoms. They had started after she had moved to the house. It had been newly renovated. Perhaps something was done during construction that shouldn't have been done, or something wasn't done that should have been. Jane didn't have a clue what. She opened her laptop.

At first what she read online was discouraging. Typical sick building symptoms sounded a lot like mild allergies: runny nose, sore throat, watery eyes, and so on. But one click led to another, and soon Jane was reading about black mold. Although mold's most common effects were the typical cold-like symptoms Jane had already seen online, black mold could also affect the central nervous system. The list of possible symptoms made Jane sit back and say, "Whoa."

POOR CONCENTRATION, DEPRESSION, IRRITABILITY, CONFUSION, SLEEP DISORDERS, ANXIETY, HALLUCINATIONS

This list could explain nearly all of Megan Larsen's problems. Conditions stemming from mold contamination were almost never correctly diagnosed by physicians initially, which might be why Megan's doctor hadn't picked it up.

There was something else Jane wanted to check. Howard Borg had made Jane suspicious about what he might be capable of, both because he was a creep and because he had expertise in cybersecurity.

She tried searching about cyberstalking, so common apparently it now had earned its own compound noun. But it had to do with stalking and harassing people online. Cyberstalking was often accompanied by real-life stalking, which might account for Megan's feeling of being watched but not for any of her other complaints. Jane read on about cyberbullying and doxing. It was horrifying but didn't help her understanding of Megan's case.

Outside Jane's office windows, the sun dipped lower in the sky. The days might still be hot, but they were getting shorter. At a little after five-thirty she heard the click of her backdoor lock turning and then footsteps in the kitchen.

"I'm in here!" she called.

"Be there in a minute." Harry Welch's voice, as always, was deep and reassuring. Despite being far down the rabbit hole into the dark side of the online world, Jane relaxed her shoulders and let out an involuntary sigh. She heard the refrigerator door open and close, the chime from a pair of wineglasses as they were pulled from a high shelf. Jane had needed reading glasses for more than two decades and her knees creaked whenever she stood up, but her hearing was still excellent.

Harry appeared in the archway between Jane's office and her dining room carrying a tray holding two wineglasses, a bottle of Montepulciano, a basket of crackers, and a cutting board with three types of cheese. "You close to finishing up?"

"I'm done." Jane closed her browser and shut down her laptop.

Harry was a widower. His beloved Elda had died six years earlier. He'd spent most of his life in a successful marriage and was close to his two grown sons, who lived near him and had children of their own.

Jane's story couldn't have been more different. More than thirty years earlier, her ex-husband, Francis, then an assistant professor and now a full professor of economics at Harvard, had talked her into taking out a huge home-equity loan, allegedly to remodel their entirely satisfactory kitchen. Then he had left, moving in with and eventually marrying his department secretary but only after depositing the cash from the loan in a bank account held only in his name.

Jane had thrown herself into finding a job, then building a career and raising their son, Jonathan. A judge had eventually made Francis pay back the loan, but it had been touch and go there for a while. Her house, the only home Jonathan had ever known, had hung in the balance.

Jane had not had so much as a thought about a romantic relationship from the day her marriage ended until a little over a year ago, when Harry had walked into Peet's for a coffee date he'd set up online at the urging of his sons. Jane was there under false pretenses. She thought she was vetting potential dates for Phyllis. It had all been a setup, though neither Jane nor Harry had known at the time. As for her son, Jonathan, he and Jane had not spoken for more than ten years. It was a source of daily heartbreak for her. Parenting was the one area in her life where she had most desperately wanted to succeed. And the one where she had most spectacularly failed.

"Shall we sit outside? It's cooled off a bit." Harry inclined his head toward the door that led from Jane's office to the garden.

"Sure. I would say we should enjoy these days while they last, but it feels as though summer will never end."

They sat in the comfortable chairs on Jane's patio, enjoying the waning light. "You look beat," Harry said. "Busy day?"

He was a handsome man of Jane's own age. His mustache was entirely white and great white hairs grew in his impressive dark brows. He wore a neat plaid sport shirt and khaki slacks. He would have looked at home in a law office with either Andy Bromfield or Ben Fox, a senior partner, éminence grise. He kept fit with aggressive games of tennis, indoors in winter and outdoors in the months without an "r" in them. His love of the game wasn't something they shared. Jane preferred her mornings in her garden.

"New case," Jane answered.

"Tell me," Harry said.

Jane glanced at the windows of Megan's second floor, which were the only ones she could see over the fence. They were dark, but she lowered her voice just the same. She and Harry often discussed her cases. Her friend Helen had assured her that spouses and romantic partners were special exceptions to promises of confidentiality, unless such discretion was specifically requested by the confidante. Jane's cases were usually problems with family members, service providers, and neighbors. Megan's problems were deeper and more threatening. Nonetheless, Jane craved Harry's wisdom. She decided she would tell him about the case but wouldn't disclose that the client was her neighbor to protect them all.

"A young woman has approached me," she began. It took a while to explain the case and her activities that morning. Harry listened appreciatively, occasionally putting more Roquefort on a Triscuit or sipping his wine. He was a deep and thoughtful listener, a quality Jane treasured.

"The further I get into it, the more I'm convinced there is nothing wrong with that young woman," Jane concluded.

Harry considered. "You're hardly in a position to make that judgment, are you?"

"I'm not a doctor, no." Jane lifted her glass and drank. "I realize that hiding how crazy you are from friends and family can be part of being crazy. I'm sure she's not as perfect as she comes off. No one is. But hallucinations, losing time, and paranoia are symptoms of a serious mental illness, and that just doesn't compute in this case."

Harry fixed another cracker and chewed it slowly. "If it's not in her head, where are the symptoms coming from?"

"That's what I've been trying to figure out. I think it might have to do with her house."

Harry listened again while Jane reprised her research on toxic mold.

"Seems possible," he said.

"I've also been wondering if it could be related to her home security system. It's quite an elaborate setup."

"It's not my area, per se." Harry had been circumspect about his former profession. He'd told Jane he had worked for the federal government and had traveled a great deal, which kept him away from his family, something he now regretted. But that was all he would say. "It could be," he continued slowly, "that someone might have hacked into her system."

"I tried to see if it's possible," Jane said. "But I couldn't figure out what to call it. It's not cyberstalking. That's something else."

"I believe it's called digital or cyber gaslighting." Harry sat back in his chair, his arms folded across his belly.

"Gaslighting?"

Harry nodded. "Named originally for the play and the movie *Gaslight*, in which a husband dims and brightens the gas lights in their home to convince his wife she's going crazy. Now technology has moved on. Typically, one spouse or partner takes much more interest in the home security system. They get it installed, program all the options, and so on. The other spouse knows only how to enter the home and turn the alarm on and off. It's not their thing. They break up, and the ex starts a campaign of harassment from anywhere in the world from their phone."

"That's horrifying," Jane said.

"This person could turn up the heat at night until your client wakes up and then drop it down," Harry explained. "They could move the digital clocks forward and then back, hence the sense that she's losing time."

Jane's excitement rose. This could be it.

"Whoever it is would need to be watching her," Harry said. "To know when to change the temperature or flash the lights or move the clocks."

"The cameras! I saw one in the kitchen and one in the garage. I'll bet they're all over the house. If someone has hacked into the system—"

"It's almost always the ex," Harry said.

"I don't see him as the type. I would start with the creepy online date guy I met today. He has a technology security business."

"Seems as good a place as any. But you should explore the mold thing too. You can figure it out." Harry's confidence in her was reassuring, but Jane wasn't sure it was well placed. She didn't know the first thing about modern security systems or sick houses.

They cleared away the cheese and crackers and started dinner. Harry cooked salmon while Jane made a salad. Jane stole glances at him as he bent over, concentrating on the fish. She wouldn't have described herself as lonely before he'd arrived, but now Jane felt a wave of gratitude to have him in her life. Cooking with Harry was companionable and relaxing, and if, while helping to clean up, he occasionally put pots back in the wrong cabinet and utensils in the wrong drawer, it was a small price to pay.

Chapter Nine

Later that evening, while Harry watched the Red Sox play the Toronto Blue Jays on TV, Jane went to her desk and searched the web for information about digital gaslighting. She was prepared to be horrified by what she read, and she wasn't wrong. Smart home technology could be harnessed by abusers to destabilize their victims, convincing them they were going crazy. Everything that had happened in Megan's house was chronicled in one article or another, along with other abuses, such as door keycodes changing every day and speakers blaring music at all hours. The perpetrators were almost always ex-partners. The motive was power and control.

Jane pulled from her pocketbook the card Megan had given her and dialed the cell number.

"Megan Larsen."

"Megan, it's Jane. Where are you?"

"In my office in town. Late night tonight. We have a

big meeting with an important client the day after tomorrow, and we're all here working hard to be ready."

"I have a quick question, if that's okay." Jane needed to be respectful of Megan's time. "Have you ever experienced any of your problems when you were away from your house?"

"What do you mean?" Megan sounded sharp, but Jane knew she was eager, not rude.

"Do you ever lose time or hear voices when you're in your office? Have you ever woken up drenched in sweat or seeing flashing lights when you've slept in a hotel room?"

"I never thought." Then the words came in a rush. "Oh my gosh, how could I have been so stupid? But when I'm at work, which I mostly am when I'm not at my house, I have client meetings and closing deadlines that mean I have to be aware of every minute of every day. So I never thought . . . I never stopped to think . . ."

"So that's a no," Jane confirmed.

"What have you found?"

Jane itched to tell her but restrained herself. This was not a time to jump to conclusions. "I'm not ready to report yet. I need two things to continue. Can you give me the name of your home security company and the name of the developer who sold you your house?"

"You think that's it? It has to do with my house?"

"I need to do more research."

"Okay, but I won't lie. You've given me hope."

"Let's not get ahead of ourselves."

"The security system was installed and is serviced by a company called Acme in Fresh Pond."

"Do you know a lot about the system?"

Megan laughed. "Hardly. I had to have a technician come out and tell me how to use it after I moved in. Wait. I have his card in my wallet. His name is Justin Vreeland." Megan read off the phone number. "The developer I bought the house from is Clark Kinnon, of Clark Kinnon Homes. His number's in my phone. Hold on." Megan came back on the line and rattled off the number.

Jane recognized the developer's name from the sign that had stood out on the muddy lawn next door through the entire renovation. "Let's plan to get together tomorrow when you get home from work."

"Yes, yes. Please. Of course. Thank you."

Chapter Ten

In the morning, Harry kissed Jane good-bye and returned to his own house to change for a tennis game. He'd left a toothbrush in the holder in her bathroom, but since he kept no clothes aside from sleeping things at her house, he always had to go home to shower and dress. He had pointed this out to Jane a few times, but when there'd been no response he'd let it drop.

Jane didn't understand why she resisted. Harry had been staying over for six months, more and more frequently if she was honest. But having his clothes at her house felt like a big step. She resisted feeling rushed, though at their age taking it slow was ridiculous.

"You're playing tennis outdoors?" Jane asked him. The day was as hot as all the ones preceding it. The media reported continuously on the length of the drought and the record-breaking heat.

"I'll be fine."

"Drink plenty of water." It was a ridiculous suggestion. Of course he would, but she needed to remind him anyway.

"Yes, ma'am."

When he was gone, Jane dressed and ate breakfast. She dawdled, wondering what it would be like to have Harry there every morning. Was she ready for that? Was he? "Enough," she said aloud. There was no point in pondering answers to questions that hadn't been asked. She went to the desk in her office. It was Wednesday, an office hours day for her. While she waited to see if anyone turned up she called Megan's alarm company.

A chipper female voice picked up. "Acme Security."

"Hello. My name is Jane Darrowfield. I'm interested in installing one of your security systems in my home. A friend of mine recommended I speak to Justin Vreeland, one of your technicians."

"I'm sorry. Technician Vreeland is out on a call. Our technicians don't really speak to prospects. They're too busy servicing existing accounts. Perhaps I can help you."

Jane settled into her seat. "Perhaps you can. And you are?"

"Agnes Antonucci."

Her voice was too young for an Agnes. Perhaps she was named for a grandmother or great-aunt. Or perhaps she was a generationally appropriately named Agnes with a young voice. Or Agnes was one of those names that had cycled back, and Jane had somehow missed it.

"I'm interested in a system with some specific capabilities," Jane told her. "In addition to an alarm system to alert me if someone enters my house, I'd like to be able to control some household functions remotely. Is that something you do?"

"Yes, absolutely. Our Homesafe app allows you to control many household systems from your phone." Agnes sounded pleased to have such a ready answer.

"Can I control my home heating system from my phone?"

"Absolutely."

Which might explain Megan waking up drenched in the night. "Can I open and close my garage door?"

"Certainly, as long as your garage door opener is electronic, of course."

"Can I control my television?"

"All of your televisions," Agnes reassured her.

"Not only turn the TV on and off, but can I access the cable box and change things like the time showing on the clock?"

"Yes, yes."

"I assume I can access the cameras that are part of the system from my phone," Jane said.

"Like a nanny cam? Of course," Agnes answered.

"And can I speak through the system to someone in my house?"

Agnes was losing patience with the extended interrogation. "Perhaps you'd like to have one of our salespeople call on you and assess your home. We could give you an estimate for installation. What is your address?"

"Forty Birchwood Lane, West Cambridge."

"We do quite a lot of work in your neighborhood." Hearing Jane's address seemed to reignite Agnes's enthusiasm for the call.

"I'm not quite ready for an estimate," Jane said. "I'm

concerned about the security of my security system, so to speak. Could a stranger gain access to it and change my heat settings or open my garage door?"

"No way. An outsider cannot gain access to your system to manipulate those things." Agnes sounded insulted to have been asked.

"There's no way?" Jane made her skepticism clear.

"No way," Agnes confirmed. "First of all, there's the system itself, which is made by one of the largest, highest quality technology companies in America. They test the system. When we install one of their systems, we test it too. Not just initially, but quarterly on random dates. We have our own team whose job it is to try to break into the system and report any breaches or weaknesses."

"So there are ways." Jane had initially assumed Agnes was a receptionist, then later decided she had a customer service or sales role of some kind. But Agnes spoke with such confidence and pride in the company, Jane wondered if she was a manager there, or even an owner. How big was Acme Security anyway? Jane would have to find out.

"We've never had one breach," Agnes insisted. "Not ever."

"Never?" Why was Jane's bank always sending her new credit cards because of "fraud control," and why had some huge retailers and service companies had customer information stolen? It seemed impossible that not a single Acme security system had been breached.

"Finally, there's our third tier of security," Agnes continued. "Our system constantly monitors our clients' logs to make sure there has been no unauthorized access. It would alert us immediately were that to occur. It never has."

"Then how do you know it works?"

"Because we test it regularly like everything else." Agnes's tone was quite short.

But Jane kept trying. "Is there any other way, other than a system breach, that someone could gain control of a system?"

"Sure!" Agnes's chipper tone returned. "When we investigate, one hundred percent of the time we discover the issue is human error."

"What kind of human error?"

"People give out the codes to contractors or cleaning companies or dog walkers and then fail to change them after the relationship ends. Or parents, siblings, or adult children." Agnes was on a roll. "Sometimes, the house changes hands and the owner doesn't change the codes, so not only do all the people they've given the codes to have them, all the people the previous owner gave the codes to have them as well."

"If I had a technician, like Justin Vreeland, out to my house to teach me how to use the system, would he automatically change the codes as a part of the service?"

"He would teach you how to change the codes, but you'd have to follow through."

Jane thought. "I get that a lot of people might be able to get into the house, but I'm not asking about that. To change the thermostat or flash the lights, wouldn't a person have to have access via a smartphone?"

Agnes paused. "That would be correct. And you can't download our app without a unique code we give you, different from the alarm or keypad codes. But some people do share the code for the app—spouses, live-ins, roommates, and so on."

"Can you tell from the logs if a phone other than the owner's accesses and manipulates the system?"

Agnes grew wary. "We'll send a salesperson out who can answer your questions in detail."

Fair enough. Jane was a little surprised by how much Agnes had said. "Thank you. I'll be calling some other companies as well and will get back to you if I want to move forward with Acme."

Agnes was done with her. "Thank you and have a good day." *Click.*

Chapter Eleven

After Jane hung up with Acme, she called a home in-spector whose website said he specialized in identi-fying sick buildings. He wasn't there, so she left her name and number on his voice mail. His message, even his voice, sounded expensive.

She also called Ben Fox, the ex-boyfriend, to see if Megan had ever given him the codes to her security sys-tem. He didn't pick up and, on reflection, Jane was glad. If he was gaslighting Megan, he was hardly likely to admit he had her security system app on his phone. Better to ask Megan if she'd ever given him the special code to download it.

By the time Jane had completed her calls office hours were over. She got in her car and went off to visit the for-mer owner of Megan's house, the developer who had flipped the property. She knew where to find the Clark Kinnon Homes office because the newish, brick two-story building happened to be between Jane's house and Irma Brittleson's, a route she traveled whenever the bridge game was at Irma's place. The sign in front of Kinnon's building was in the same fonts and colors as the one that had been on the lawn next door all those months.

Jane parked in the small lot in front of the building and entered through a glass door. A harassed-looking receptionist stared at a computer monitor on her messy desk. A placard that read GLORIA ZINN hung precariously on the corner of the desk, ready to be pushed off at any second by an avalanche of paper.

"I'm here to see Mr. Kinnon," Jane announced.

"You don't have an appointment." It wasn't a question.

"I do not," Jane affirmed. "Is he here?"

Gloria Zinn sighed and stood up. She was skinny as a stick and her curly hair stuck up from her scalp as if it was trying to escape. "I'll check. What can I say this is in regard to?"

"The property at 42 Birchwood Lane. I'm here on behalf of the owner. We're investigating whether the house might have sick building syndrome."

As Jane expected, that gambit brought an immediate response. Gloria Zinn skittered down a dark hallway, and seconds later Clark Kinnon followed her back to the front desk. He held out his hand. "I'm Clark. How can I help you?"

Jane recognized him from months of coming and going as he'd overseen the renovation at the property next door. He was a medium-height man and very square. Square head emphasized by close-cropped brown hair. Square shoulders emphasized by the cut of his sports jacket. Even his manicured fingernails were squared. Not a bad-looking man, despite the squareness. In his midforties, Jane guessed.

Jane took the offered hand and shook. "I'm here on behalf of Megan Larsen, who bought the property you fl— renovated on Birchwood Lane in Cambridge. Some things have come up at the house, and I wanted to chat about its history." Much less threatening. No use of the words *sick building*.

"Of course. Come in." He gestured down the unlit hall toward his doorway. At the same time he looked directly at Ms. Zinn, and something passed between them wordlessly. Jane followed him into the darkness. Were they trying to save on electricity, keep the place cooler, or what? He ushered Jane into his office. "Please sit down and tell me how I can help you."

"I live next door at 40 Birchwood," Jane said when she was seated. "I watched your renovation with admiration, and now that I've been inside the house visiting Ms. Larsen, I'm even more impressed." No need to mention she'd trooped through the open house, the very definition of a lookie-loo.

"I know your house," Kinnon said. "Lovely bones. If you ever want to sell—"

Jane's back stiffened. She wasn't unrealistic. She couldn't stay in her home forever. But the thought of this man tearing out the beautiful molding, the staircase, the built-in bookcases that surrounded the fireplace, every bit of detail that gave her home its character . . . "I have no plans at the moment," she said. "I wonder what you can tell me about number forty-two. Was it in poor condition when you purchased it?"

"Typical of its age and type, I would say. Of course the

Baxters were quite elderly. They'd lived there forever and had never done anything to the property beyond basic upkeep."

"But you saw the potential."

He squared his square shoulders. "Name of the game. Undervalued property in a prime location. That's what we do. Your neighborhood is golden."

He glanced toward the door. As if on cue, Ms. Zinn appeared and placed a piece of printer paper on his desk. Even upside down, Jane could read the note scrawled across it: *Megan Larsen says okay to talk.*

"Thank you, Gloria." She withdrew, and Kinnon turned to Jane. "Now, why don't you tell me what this is really about?"

Jane cleared her throat. "Ms. Larsen has had some issues with the house, and I've come to get some background. You chose the company to install the security system. Why Acme?"

He relaxed visibly. Acme apparently wasn't a controversial choice. "I bring them in on all my residential deals. Agnes Antonucci, the owner, is great to work with, and they install only absolute top-of-the-line systems, a necessity in neighborhoods like yours."

Jane was surprised. She would have described her part of Cambridge as quiet and safe, hardly requiring heavy-duty security. "Why is that?"

"Because of the likely buyers. These are people of significant means. They have several homes and therefore are frequently not in residence at the property for months at a time. They may have children attending school locally who could be the target of kidnappers. These buyers expect the very best."

Ah, the Russian oligarchs, Middle Eastern royalty, Chinese billionaires, and Eurotrash whom the bridge club had discussed. "Megan wasn't the buyer you expected."

He smiled. "No, not at all, but I was more than happy to take her money. All cash, no inspections. Just as I would have expected from my target buyer."

So Megan had paid cash. That was a lot of money for a lawyer in her midthirties and not yet a partner. Jane wondered where it had come from. "Did you happen to keep the security codes for the house when you sold it?"

"I assume Ms. Larsen changed them. I did have the app with the codes in it on my phone, but I haven't used it since the house was sold."

"Did you give the codes to anyone else?"

"Lots of people. After the system was installed I gave the codes to enter the house and disarm the system to my general contractor, and I assume he gave them to some of the subcontractors and maybe even suppliers if they needed to get into the house."

"Did you give any of them the code to download the phone app?"

He drew his brows together. "I doubt it. I don't see why any of them would have needed it. I used it myself only if one of those guys forgot to lock the doors behind him."

"What about the condition of the house?" Jane asked. "Did you do any mold abatement during the renovation? Find any toxins? Use any new type of materials or finishings?"

The room suddenly felt colder. "What are you implying?" Kinnon stood and leaned across the desk, his face flushed red. "If you so much as even hint to anyone that I sell buildings that are not up to the highest standards, far beyond what is required by code, I will ruin your reputation and your life. This conversation is at an end. Gloria!"

Gloria Zinn's footsteps echoed down the hallway until she screeched to a halt in front of the office. "I'll see you out," she said to Jane.

And that was that.

Chapter Twelve

"I have two theories about what's going on." Jane and Megan were seated at Megan's white kitchen island with the shiny white countertop. They each had a glass mug of tea in front of them. Jane lifted the mug. It was heavy and obviously expensive. How did an unmarried woman come by such things? Was this another way Megan was signaling she didn't need a man, or a truck-load of wedding presents, to live the life she wanted?

"What do you think is going on? It's my house, isn't it? That's why you asked if I ever had my symptoms away from home." Megan leaned toward Jane, eager for the answer.

"Yes, I think the problem may be your house," Jane said.

"But what? How?"

"There are two possibilities. It could be either or both. The first is some kind of environmental issue."

Megan sat back on her barstool, surprised. "Environmental issue? Like what?"

"The house was gut renovated before you bought it. There may have been some kind of material used in the renovation. Or there might have been some shortcuts taken, things covered up."

"Like mold." Megan was the A student, getting ahead of the teacher.

"Like black mold," Jane confirmed.

"I didn't have a home inspection," Megan said. "I feel like an idiot." In the bidding frenzies that had accompanied the steep increase in demand in their neighborhood, inspections were frequently waived, especially in renovated properties.

"You need a specialist." Jane took a deep breath. "We need to get inspectors in here to examine the major systems for toxins. The worst that happens is we rule it out."

Megan nodded, ready to get down to business. "Can you handle this for me? Set up the appointments with the inspectors and let them in? And if work has to be done, can you manage it? It's crazy busy at the firm right now."

"Of course," Jane said. "Same hourly fee. I'd like to see this through to resolution too."

"I'll give you the codes for the alarm system so you can let the inspectors and any repair people in." Megan said it routinely, as if giving away access to her security system was something she did without hesitation.

"Of course. Write them down for me."

Megan took a blank index card off the desk and wrote down four series of numbers, labeling them. She knew the first three by heart, but she had to copy the last one from a paper she retrieved from the drawer in the kitchen desk.

Jane studied the paper. Megan had listed her garage
door code, the code for the interior door from the garage
to the kitchen, the code to shut off the alarm, and the code
to download the phone app. "You gave me the code to put
your system on my phone."

"I figured you should have everything in case you
need it. You're right next door. You might want to turn off
the alarm when you see a repair truck turning into the
driveway instead of waiting until you get over here. It's
good for stuff like that."

"How many people have you given these codes to?"
Jane asked.

Megan was more curious than alarmed. "Why?"

"That's my other theory. I think someone may have
hacked into your home security system."

"Oh my gosh." Megan stared at the camera on the
kitchen wall, horrified.

"Who have you given the codes to?"

Megan stared up at the shiny copper pans hanging
above the island, trying to remember. "Andy, of course,"
she said slowly. "And my dad."

"Your dad is local?"

"He lives in Boston."

Why hadn't Jane thought to talk to him about any recent changes in Megan's behavior? Why hadn't Megan
suggested him?

Megan continued. "The kid who looks after Wembly
when I travel. The house cleaners, the dry cleaner's deliv-
ery person, the gardener because he has to come through
the garage to get to the backyard." The words came out in
a rush. "The guy who came in to service my heating system when I was at work." Megan's eyes were wide. She
realized how careless she'd been.

"Did you give the codes to Ben?"

She hesitated. "Maybe. Probably. When I moved in. But Ben would never do anything to hurt me. I'm sure of it."

"I'm not accusing anyone, just trying to get a sense of what we're dealing with. I'm particularly interested in people who might have this last code, the one to download the phone app."

"I don't know." Megan was increasingly upset. "I didn't give it out, I don't think. Except when I first moved in and didn't understand how the system worked. I might have given it out then without realizing. Would they need the app to hack the system?"

"It would be the simplest way to do all the things that were done to you," Jane said. "Turn up the thermostat, flash the lights, open the garage door, turn on the TV downstairs, change the time on the DVR."

"And that's what's causing my problems?" A tear slid down Megan's cheek.

"We can't be sure yet, but I think it may be. I know it's a lot to think your privacy may have been violated in such a horrible way."

"It's not that." Megan wiped away tears with her fingers. "I'm just so . . . just so relieved. This means so much to me to hear you say I'm not crazy." Then she broke down.

Jane got up from the stool and retrieved a box of tissues off the built-in desk.

"Thank you." Megan pulled one out and dabbed at her gray eyes, still made up from her day at work. "I wasn't entirely honest with you. It's true, I didn't want my firm or my insurance company to know I might have a serious mental illness, but it's not because of the partnership. It's because I hope to adopt a baby." Megan blew her upturned nose. "I've done all the research. I'm ready to move forward. But obviously if I am seriously mentally ill, I can't do it." She sniffed, slowly pulling herself together. "My mother was crazy. It made my childhood a hell on earth. I would never do that to another child."

Would Jane have ruled out mental illness so quickly if she'd known of Megan's family history? She didn't think so. "How is your mother now?"

"She's gone," Megan said, looking down at the white counter. "She died when I was seven."

"I'm so sorry."

Megan blew her nose again and tried to smile. "I can't thank you enough for all your help. This is unbelievable."

"Let's not get ahead of ourselves. We still have to prove it," Jane said. "One more thing. Turn off the security cameras. For the time being. Until we figure this out."

"Okay." Megan looked at the kitchen wall again and shuddered. "I thought the cameras were stupid when I bought the place, but then I got kind of addicted to watching Wembly and talking to him when I was at work."

At the door, Jane gave Megan a hug. "Will you be okay?" It was terrible to think some unknown person might be watching.

"Yes. Thinking I was crazy was way worse than this." Megan gave a little laugh. "To think I came to you fearful someone was after me, and now you're telling me to turn off my security cameras."

"Just for the time being," Jane repeated.

"I'll do it right now," Megan promised.

Chapter Thirteen

The next morning, Jane was awakened by the *brrruppp* of her cell phone on the nightstand. She picked up the phone, staring sleepily at it, her eyes coming into focus. A familiar name appeared on the screen. She pressed the green button to answer and sat straight up.

"Detective Alvarez. How can I help you at"—Jane squinted at the tiny numbers on the phone—"nine-twenty in the morning?" She'd slept in. She'd given up setting her alarm clock when she'd retired, and that morning Harry had snuck off early to spend the day with his grandsons. She had slumbered on.

"Hello, Jane." Alvarez's voice was friendly, though thoroughly in charge. "This isn't a social call. I'm at the house next door to yours."

"Megan's house? Is she okay?" Jane was out of bed and across the room, looking out the window. Two cars were parked in Megan's drive. Alvarez's unmarked, official Cambridge Police Department sedan and a bright blue Prius. Detective Alvarez stood on Megan's front steps, his cell phone pressed to his ear.

"She's not here," Alvarez said, his voice still calm. Through the window, Jane watched his lips move. "I'm here with a colleague who insists she is missing."

"Missing!"

"Apparently, she failed to show at an important meeting at work, and her cell phone is on the kitchen counter." He paused. "I'm calling because your name and number are written on the blackboard here. Do you know where she is?"

"I'll be right there."

Jane dressed as fast as she could. Alvarez was at the open door as she hurried across Megan's front lawn. Andy Bromfield stood behind him. "I'm glad you're here," Alvarez said when she reached the front steps.

Jane entered the big open room. "What's this about Megan?"

"She had an important client meeting this morning, which she no-showed. Mr. Bromfield is most insistent there is a problem. He arrived at the house and found she wasn't here. I was in the neighborhood, so I took the call."

"You don't understand." Andy's tone was insistent. "Megan would never, ever miss a meeting this important. Not with her partnership at the firm on the line. Not in any circumstance. Even if there was an emergency, she would have called me. Or called the client to let them know. Someone." His voice had risen throughout his explanation, louder and higher and more panic-stricken. "You need to look for her."

Alvarez put his hands on his belt, opening his sports

jacket and showing a great deal of crisp, white cotton shirt. His hair was dark, almost black. He was fit and well built, the model of a no-nonsense detective, except for his baby face, which made him look a decade younger than his thirty-seven years.

"Mr. Bromfield," he said. "The Cambridge Police Department is not in the habit of looking for healthy adults who have missed one business meeting. If we did, we would do nothing else."

Andy was disheveled, his curly hair mussed, his glasses askew, his tie loosened. "You don't understand. This meeting was very, very important. The whole department has been preparing for it for weeks. Megan wouldn't have missed it. She's as type A as they come, an overachiever, compulsively responsible."

Alvarez smiled. "So is half of Cambridge."

"And"—Andy pointed dramatically at Jane—"she hired this private detective three days ago."

"I never said I was a private detective," Jane said quietly.

"I'm sure you didn't." Alvarez knew her better than that. They'd worked together several times before, mostly on smaller things—elder fraud, identity theft—but one time on a murder. "Why did Ms. Larsen hire you?" Alvarez asked her.

Jane stood, rooted to the spot, both men staring at her. She wasn't worried about disclosure. She trusted Alvarez, and Megan trusted Andy. She was worried about how to frame the answer and what might happen, or not happen, based on what she said. Alvarez had said the Cambridge Police didn't look for healthy missing adults, but what about unhealthy, mentally unstable ones? Would that change the priority?

"Ms. Larsen had some concerns," Jane began.

"Obviously," Alvarez agreed. Andy shifted in his loafers, impatient.

"For her safety," Jane clarified.

"See!" Andy hissed, which brought a hand gesture of impatience from Alvarez.

"Ms. Larsen felt unsafe," Alvarez confirmed.

"Among other things."

Alvarez was still rolling his hand in a speed-it-up motion, so Jane spit it out. "She came to me initially because she was worried she might be mentally ill."

"No!" Andy almost shouted. "Megan is as sane as anyone in this room."

Jane put a hand on his forearm, hoping to calm him, but he jumped away from her, quivering with anxiety. "She wasn't sure if she was ill, which is why she came to me. And why I talked to you, Andy."

"I don't understand," Alvarez said. "You're not a doctor."

"Megan didn't believe she was ill, but she was scared by her symptoms. She wanted me to get to the bottom of them."

"And did you get to the bottom of them?" Alvarez asked.

"Not entirely. But I came to believe Ms. Larsen was being gaslighted by someone using her home security system."

"WHAT?" Andy did shout that time.

Jane repeated what she had said and described Megan's symptoms, the temperature changes, flashing lights, time jumps, and voices.

"And you're convinced all this was caused by someone manipulating her home security system?" Alvarez asked.

"I'm not certain. It was a working theory. I'm also concerned about household toxins, sick building syndrome. I haven't ruled anything definitively in or out."

"Including mental illness," Alvarez confirmed.

"THERE IS NOTHING WRONG WITH MEGAN." Andy was bug-eyed by this point. Veins bulged in his forehead.

"As you said, I'm not in a position to diagnose."

Alvarez's eyes traveled up to the camera high on the kitchen wall.

"You won't see anything there," Jane advised him.

"Why not?"

"Because I told her to turn the cameras off. Yesterday evening."

All three of them were standing there, absorbing that bit of information, when the front door flew open and a distinguished-looking man in his sixties walked in. "What's going on here?" he demanded.

Alvarez stepped forward. "Detective Alvarez, Cambridge Police Department. I assume you're Mr. Larsen."

"You called *him*?" Andy seemed dumbfounded.

"His name is on the bulletin board." Alvarez pointed to a small business card tacked beside Megan's vision collage. "I called him when I stepped outside to call Mrs. Darrowfield. I assumed from the surname he was related." Alvarez turned to the man. "You're Megan's father?"

"Guilty as charged." Larsen had a full head of white hair, slicked back in a way that seemed old-fashioned even to Jane, and a handsome, masculine face. Bright white

French cuffs and ebony cuff links peeked out from the sleeves of his gray suit. He was tall and thin; the weight he had put on with age had gathered in a single place, a round potbelly. He looked like the sort of man who would tell you what brand of scotch to order, whether you asked him or not.

"Why didn't you tell me you were going to call *him*?" Andy twitched with anger.

"Mr. Larsen is apparently Megan's next of kin, and you are . . ." Alvarez hesitated. "A work colleague."

"I'm her *friend*," Andy insisted.

"Her friend, then." Alvarez addressed Mr. Larsen. "As I told you briefly over the phone, your daughter missed an important business meeting this morning. Her cell phone is here in the house, but Megan is not. Mr. Bromfield felt this was most out of character."

Larsen stood a bit apart from them. When they'd talked, Jane, Alvarez, and Andy had formed the corners of an equidistant triangle. Larsen had turned them into a weird rhombus, which made the room feel off-kilter.

"I don't think it's out of character at all," Larsen said. "I think it's very much in character. Megan is highly strung, a perfectionist. Sometimes the pressure gets to be too much and she needs a break, a time-out. I'm sure that's what's happening now with this partnership decision coming up at her firm."

"I've never seen behavior like that," Andy protested.

"You don't know her like I do." Mr. Larsen's tone was authoritative in a way that suggested he was used to being in charge. "When she was a child, Megan had to be treated for stress on numerous occasions. When it got bad, she would sleepwalk."

"Treated how?" Alvarez asked.

"By a child psychologist. What else would I mean?" Larsen was dismissive.

A child psychologist? Megan had said nothing to Jane about previous treatment. Would sleepwalking explain some of her symptoms? The lost time? Awakening to flashing lights? Perhaps she was turning the lights on and off in her sleep, waking herself up. Had Jane got Megan all wrong?

"Where is Ms. Larsen's mother?" Alvarez asked.

"She's de—" Jane started.

"No idea," her father answered. "We've been divorced for almost thirty years."

"Megan's mother is alive?" Jane was stunned.

"Of course she is. At least no one's told me she isn't, and I'm sure I would have heard."

"Could Megan have gone to her?" Alvarez asked.

"No!" Both Mr. Larsen and Andy Bromfield said it at once.

"Megan is not with her mother, I assure you," Larsen said. Jane wanted to know more, but it wasn't the time to ask. Larsen scanned the room. "Is the cat here?"

Alvarez glanced toward the bowls on the floor by the kitchen island. "I haven't seen a cat since I arrived. Excuse me." Alvarez stepped out the front door. Jane could see him through the window, speaking into his cell phone.

"Wembly!" Andy climbed the stairs to the second floor, calling for the cat. "Wembly!"

Jane found a can of cat food in a kitchen cabinet and opened it using the electric can opener. In her experience the whir of the machine was a siren call for dogs and cats alike. Nothing. She dumped the contents into his clean bowl, hoping to entice him.

Andy came back from upstairs. "No cat." Alvarez had rejoined them as well.

"You see," Mr. Larsen said, "if Megan has made arrangements for the cat, she's fine."

The sound of slamming car doors came from in front of the house, and seconds later two uniformed officers came through the front door—a petite red-haired woman and a tall bald man.

"Search the house and grounds for any signs of the owner and anything that might have happened to her," Alvarez told them. "And keep your eyes out for a cat."

The male officer opened the door to the garage. "No car here, sir."

"She doesn't own one," Andy said.

"She's too nervous to drive," Larsen added, which seemed a little gratuitous, but Jane supposed it did tell Alvarez something about Megan's character. The same officer went into the study, which was on the other side of the staircase, the only separate room on the first floor. "Laptop's here," he called.

"You see," Andy said. "Megan would never go anywhere without her laptop and her phone."

"Unless she was trying to get away from it all," Larsen contradicted.

Jane could hear the female officer upstairs, opening doors and calling, "Here, kit, kit, kit." The officer who'd searched the study went down to the basement. "Here, puss, puss, puss." He stomped back up and went out to the backyard. It was all done with efficiency and speed.

"Nothing, sir," the female officer reported when they'd returned to the main room. The other nodded his head in agreement.

"Thank you, you can go." Alvarez turned to Larsen. "So I take it you don't want to file a report or have us follow up?"

"Absolutely not." Larsen didn't seem to have a hint of doubt. "Andy here and I can keep an eye out for her."

"Okay." Alvarez started for the door. "Mr. Bromfield, you let me in."

"I'll lock up," Andy assured him. "I have the alarm code."

"I'll lock up." Larsen was quick to assert his authority. "I'm her father. I have the alarm code too."

Chapter Fourteen

There didn't seem to be anything else to do or say, so Jane left via the front door with Andy Bromfield close on her heels. The two squad cars drove away from the curb and then Detective Alvarez pulled out of the driveway. Jane expected Andy to get in the Prius and drive away too, but instead he followed her around the hedge and up the walk to her house.

"Can I come in to talk? I'm really concerned about Megan."

"I can tell." Jane opened her front door and let him in. He trailed her to the kitchen, where she offered him something to drink.

"Tea, please, if it's not too much trouble." He smiled apologetically. "It calms me when I'm stressed."

Jane took her time making the tea, offering Andy milk, sugar, or lemon. He took the milk, nothing else. Jane did the same and led him to the living room. She settled in her favorite chair. It was a worn pink brocade, a color she no longer loved, with spots from the innumerable snacks she'd dropped while sitting in it. But it fit her perfectly, held her body like a gloved hand, kept her back straight, and had a matching ottoman. Andy sat on the pale blue couch.

"Now tell me why you're so worried," Jane said.

"You told the detective someone might have broken into Megan's home security system."

"Yes, but you didn't know that when you called the police this morning. Why did you sound the alarm the moment Megan didn't show up for the meeting?"

Andy stared down at the tea in his cup, but he didn't drink. "First of all, there's Megan missing this meeting. I don't think any of you understand how important it was. There are two ways to become a partner in a law firm. The first is to bring in your own clients, 'Make it rain,' the saying goes. The second is for an established client of the firm, a big, important one, to absolutely love you and demand to work with you. That's the situation Megan has with the client we were meeting with today. Luckily, the client loves her so much they were happy to assume she'd had some kind of family emergency, but the partner-in-charge at our firm was furious. More than that, Megan would never have missed this meeting if she could help it." Andy stopped for a moment and exhaled heavily. "Never."

"Why do you think Megan's dad didn't want to report her missing?"

"Megan's dad is the last person who would know what is going on with her or how she would behave in a particular situation." There was an angry edge to Andy's voice.

"They aren't close?"

He hesitated. "She spent her whole life trying to please him, and he's never been there for her. He's more concerned with his image than his family."

Jane watched Andy, assessing. "You don't think he cares about her."

"He cares about her, all right. He cares how her achievements reflect back on him. He's always pushed her, too hard. If any of that stuff he said about her being a nervous kid is true, it was his fault."

"What does he do for work?"

Andy looked surprised. "You don't know? He's a lawyer too, a named partner at Franklin and Larsen. He's kind of a big deal."

"Megan followed in his footsteps," Jane pointed out. "She couldn't have been too alienated from him."

Andy set the teacup back in its saucer on the coffee table. "She almost made it out. She did two years at Teach for America in Brooklyn after undergrad. I thought, Good on you, stay in New York, find another path. But when she finished there she went straight to law school. Same year I started."

Jane tried to understand this new Megan—the nervous child, the liar with a living mother—weaving this information into her initial assessment. "She didn't join her father's firm."

"She has some sense of self-preservation at least. Her work would never be good enough for him." Andy paused. "No one from our year joined Franklin and Larsen. I'm not sure they even recruited from our class, or any class since. It's a staid old firm running on its name. Or half its name. The last Franklin is deceased."

Andy sighed, his shoulders rising almost to his big ears, convenient holders for his black-framed glasses.

"Megan's relationship with her father, that's something she should talk to a psychologist about. If she even had one. I wouldn't put it past her dad to have made that up, too, just to make her look bad and keep the police from looking for her."

"Why wouldn't he want the police involved if his daughter is missing?"

Andy shrugged. "I'll be charitable and say he's worried about what a lot of publicity might do to Megan's chances for the partnership. I have to admit the timing is terrible. But what I really believe is it's about Edwin Larsen's reputation and how having your daughter look anything but perfect reflects badly."

"Then *you* believe that *he* believes Megan has gone off somewhere because of the pressure of her job," Jane clarified.

"I have to believe that. Otherwise he's even worse than I've ever thought. You'd have to be a monster to discourage the police if your daughter might actually be in trouble."

That's what Jane thought too. It was one of those situations where Andy believed he was doing the right thing raising the alarm and Edwin Larsen believed he was right to lower it. "Megan told me her mother was dead." Jane was stung by this. Even though she'd learned to view people more skeptically in her work as a professional busybody, she hadn't pegged Megan as a liar.

"She does that. It's easier." Jane watched Andy struggle to decide how much of Megan's story he should tell. "Megan's mom is an alcoholic. She drank all through Megan's early childhood. When Megan was seven, I guess it got completely out of hand. That's when her dad divorced her mom and she was put into some kind of hospital. Edwin got custody of Megan, which tells you how unfit her mom was, because he honestly could not have cared less about his kid."

"You're sure Megan isn't at her mother's?"

"There were several attempts at reconciliation by Megan and her mom, sometimes initiated by Megan but usually by her mom. But in the end, her mom always fell off the wagon, broke promises, and hurt Megan. The last one was at law school graduation. Her mother showed up roaring drunk. Megan tried to pretend it was no big deal. 'Par for the course,' she said. After that time, Megan vowed, 'Never again.' That's when she started telling people her mother was dead. It's more acceptable than being completely estranged from a parent."

The last remark struck Jane like a slap. Her son was estranged from her. Did he tell people that she was dead? "Those kinds of vows have been known to be broken."

It was Jane's most fervent hope that her son, Jonathan, would someday break a similar vow. The pain of this estrangement was something Jane carried with her every day. She woke to it and fell asleep to it. She was always aware of it, like her heartburn or her bad knees, though it was sharper and much more painful. She didn't know the reason for it, though it would be a lie to say she didn't have suspicions, conversations that she examined minutely in the hours before she fell asleep. Sometimes it was too painful to even think about.

Andy was unpersuaded. "I don't think so." He shifted on the soft couch to fully face Jane. "The thing about Megan is, she was raised by wolves. Neither of her parents had any business having a child. Her dad is an egomaniac, and her mother is a drunk. Yet Megan turned out amazing. Sometimes when she's on the phone, handling a difficult client with that easy charm of hers, I look across the office and wonder, How can you be you? How does that even happen, that she turned out to be such a fantastic person? She had a stepmother for a while. Edwin remarried. She was a good person. Maybe that explains it. Or maybe that's just the person Megan is."

"What happened to the stepmother?" Maybe his wife could persuade Edwin Larsen to go back to the police and ask them to search for his daughter.

"She *is* dead," Andy said. "I mean actually dead. Breast cancer, ten years ago."

Jane thought about all the questions she hadn't asked when she'd made her glib diagnosis that Megan wasn't mentally ill. She should have asked about her parents and prior mental health issues. She'd warned Megan she wasn't a therapist, and she certainly wasn't. On the other hand, Megan had worried she was being stalked, and now Megan was gone. *Just because you're paranoid, doesn't mean they're not out to get you.*

"Not that Megan doesn't have 'stuff,'" Andy was saying. "Everybody has 'stuff.' She was alone most of her childhood, and as a result, she's always picking up strays."

That was interesting. "Were there any new strays in Megan's life?" Jane asked.

"I'm sure there were, because there always were. Some guy comes over to fix the dishwasher, and the next thing I know, Megan's representing him in a boundary dispute he's having with his neighbor. Stuff like that happens all the time with Megan. Nobody is a stranger. Nobody's not worth caring about. Even the cat is a rescue."

Even the baby, Jane thought. In this day and age when there were many ways for a young woman on her own to have a baby, Megan planned to adopt.

"Do you really think someone broke into Megan's home security system?" Andy asked.

"I don't know. I was just getting started when this happened. Can you think of anyone who would target Megan like that?"

"No-o-ope." Andy said it slowly, unwilling to commit to the answer. "But it can't be a coincidence, can it? Someone was using her security system to harass her and then she disappeared."

"I don't know," Jane answered. Though in her bones, she did. It wasn't a coincidence. "You have the codes to get into Megan's house. Do you have them in an app on your phone?"

"I do." Andy didn't seem rattled by the question. "Megan gave me access the day after she moved in. The app is pretty convenient. She has keys for my condo, too, by the way."

"Have you checked your place since you left your office? Maybe Megan's there."

"I had my neighbor check first thing when I discovered Megan wasn't at her house. She's not at my apartment." He looked, if possible, even more worried. "That wasn't the first time you and Detective Alvarez have met," he said.

"We've worked together on a few of my previous cases," Jane admitted.

"Can you talk to him, convince him Megan's in trouble and needs help? I have never been so certain of anything."

"I'll talk to him." It was the least Jane could do. "But I'm not sure what he can do based on the say-so of a friend and a neighbor when the wishes of her next of kin are so clear."

"You can try." His eyes pleaded behind his glasses.

"I will. And I'll continue to learn what I can about the security system. While I do that, you should check in with as many of her friends as you can. Think of a story that won't alarm them but find out if anyone has any idea where she might have gone."

"I'll tell them she's on vacation and I need her for some office-related thing. I'll ask if they know where she is. They'll be surprised. Usually if Megan's away, I'm the one who knows where she is, especially since she and Ben broke up."

"It's wonderful that you and Megan have remained such close friends even though you're in this competitive situation with the partnership," Jane said.

"It's not so competitive. Megan's going to get it." Andy was being more open than the last time they'd discussed this.

"And you have no bad feelings about that?"

"I'm ambivalent at best about the partnership thing, to be honest. I'd need to come up with half a million dollars to pay for my share." Andy rolled his shoulders. "I'm not sure it's worth it."

Jane had no idea. "Half a million dollars?"

"When you become an equity partner in a law firm, you have to put up money equal to the value the other partners have invested. You share in the profits according to a complicated formula, but it can be boom and bust. Plus, you get paid only twice a year, so the cash flow is tricky when you're young and haven't built up the savings to ride it. Most days I think I'd be happier collecting a salary. It's safer and more predictable. I have other obligations, my mortgage, massive school loans."

School loans? Since Andy and Megan had gone to

school together from the elementary grades onward, Jane had assumed without thinking too much about it that Andy was the same as Megan, the child of a prosperous family, more than able to pay for his education.

Andy read her look. "Scholarship kid," he said. "All my life."

"What about the other days," Jane said. "The days when you do want the partnership?"

"I only want the best for Megan. Every day."

He loves her, Jane realized with a jolt.

At her front door, Jane gave Andy a hug. *The poor guy*, she thought. *He loves her and he's scared to death.* "We'll find her," she said with more certainty than she felt. "She'll turn up."

"She has to," Andy said. "I can't think about what life would be like if she didn't come back." And then he hugged Jane, a gentle squeeze of solidarity, and walked off toward Megan's driveway and his car.

Chapter Fifteen

Jane called Detective Alvarez as soon as Andy Bromfield left but got sent back to reception at Cambridge headquarters. He wasn't able to take a call at that moment; did she want his voice mail? Jane left a breezy message—"That was interesting this morning"—and asked for a call back.

It was too hot to work in her garden, so Jane tried to accomplish some chores around her house to distract herself. Her first task after she'd retired had been to clean out her kitchen cabinets. She discarded dozens of boxes and cans past their sell-by dates and all sorts of obscure spices bought to cook a single dish and never used again. But that had been more than two years earlier, and things were getting ahead of her again. Harry did a lot of the cooking and he'd brought some of his favorite ingredients to keep at the house. There was no room for them in the cupboards, and they sat out on a countertop like unwelcome guests. Jane pulled the trash barrel from under the sink and got down to it.

But the distraction didn't work. She kept drifting to the window on the side of the house that faced Megan's front yard, hoping a taxi or an Uber would pull up and Megan would alight, laughing, with Wembly in her arms. It didn't happen. Jane stared out the window, more and more concerned.

Andy texted several times, reporting on his calls to Megan's friends and asking if she was home. This resulted in more trips to her window, and even a walk outside to peer into Megan's windows, something she felt foolish doing but that Andy begged her to do. The big white great room in Megan's house was empty and dark. There was a sticker on the window that said ACME SECURITY. Jane had never noticed it before when she'd entered and left through the garage.

In the end, the clear-out didn't work as well as Jane had hoped. When she was done, there was still no room for Harry's stash of rubs and spices.

At a little after five o'clock she heard the distinct sound of an engine stopping in the street outside. She ran to the front door and threw it open. Never before had she been disappointed when she saw Harry Welch unbuckle his seat belt and open his car door.

"What's the matter?" As soon as Harry got close enough to see her, his face mirrored her concern.

"Come in. Let's have some wine and I'll tell you."

He opened a bottle of cabernet and they sat at her kitchen island, arms touching. It had been so long since the kitchen was updated; the countertop was green ceramic tile with white grout. When he cooked dinner, Harry groused good-naturedly about the unevenness of the island's tile and the grout's tendency to stain, but Jane loved it. It was so different from Megan's shiny white kitchen.

"The young woman I told you about yesterday, the one who might have been a victim of digital gaslighting, has disappeared," Jane started.

"Oh, for heaven's sake!" Harry's eyes opened wide. "I thought you were sick or something. That look on your face. You really had me going. Feel my heartbeat." He placed her hand on his chest. His heart was thundering away.

"Nothing like that," she assured him. "But this is serious." It took her a while to tell the whole story. She still didn't disclose Megan's name or the fact that she lived next door. Jane wasn't sure why not, except that maybe Megan would be back, safe and sound, and not happy to know that the guy who hung out at the house next door had all this backstory. "It can't be a coincidence," she finished. "She was being gaslighted by someone, and now she's gone."

"We don't know for sure that's what was happening," Harry cautioned.

"No," Jane admitted, "not for sure. But doesn't her disappearance make it more likely she was a target? And I'm the one who told her to turn off her security cameras."

"None of this is your fault, Jane."

Before she could respond, her phone bounced noisily on the hard tiles. "It's Tony Alvarez. I have to take this."

Harry nodded, took his wineglass in hand, and headed for the living room.

"So that was weird this morning," Alvarez said as soon as Jane picked up.

"Hello to you too." It was their private joke. It was in both of their natures to get right to business. Jane pictured Alvarez at his cluttered desk, pecking at his keyboard, shoveling through the paperwork that would let him go home to his wife and the two teenaged stepchildren he'd helped raise. "Is that what you put in your report? 'Weird morning'?"

"It is not. My report was three sentences long. 'Called by a colleague for a possible missing person. No suspicious circumstances. Next of kin declined to pursue.'"

"And that's it?"

Alvarez hesitated. "You agree with that Bromfield guy, right? You think Megan Larsen didn't leave of her own volition."

"The woman hired me because she thought someone was stalking her. Now she's disappeared."

"Why didn't she come to us?"

"She wasn't sure. She thought it might be her imagination. She wanted me to confirm. If I had found anything criminal, I would have sent her right to you."

"And your diagnosis was digital gaslighting."

"My theory," Jane emphasized. "Though I'm more convinced of it now."

There was silence on the end of the line for a few moments. Jane could feel Alvarez digesting what he'd heard. "We've seen a lot more of this recently. We had a training session on it last month. The victim, usually a woman, gets a court order that keeps the perpetrator, usually a man, away from her location. But from the other side of town he's still playing mind games on her. It's very hard to prove. Victims rarely have the money to hire the forensic technology experts required to confirm the harassment. Law enforcement doesn't have enough of those resources either. It's difficult for the courts to write a restraining order detailed enough to prevent every way an abuser might torment someone."

"How awful someone would use technology intended to keep you safe in that way."

"It's not the technology that creates the abuser," Alvarez said. "A security system doesn't turn the average person into a harasser. But if someone is already a controlling bully, the technology provides a new tool." Alvarez sounded grave, solemn. "Had you gotten to the point of figuring out how it was done?"

"No. I talked to a woman at the company that installed the system. She said everything that happened to Megan would be easy to do if you had their phone app plus her codes. You need a particular code to download the app." Jane felt increasingly desperate. "Is there anything you can do? Maybe if you could get the security company to give you the logs from Megan's system, you could determine if she was being gaslighted."

Alvarez chuckled. "I couldn't determine anything."

"But someone there could."

"I may know someone who owes me a favor," he admitted. "I emphasize *may*. I told you these resources are hard to come by."

"And if Megan was a victim of digital gaslighting," Jane said, "could you open a case even without her father asking you to?"

"I can, if I have any reason to believe her absence is involuntary or that she's in danger."

"I don't want to wait."

The detective didn't respond right away. "All right. Give me the name of the home security company. If Ms. Larsen isn't home or hasn't contacted a friend or relative by the morning, I'll see if the company will voluntarily hand over the logs."

"It's Acme Security in Fresh Pond. I spoke to Agnes Antonucci. I think she's the owner." Jane gave him the phone number.

"It's a long shot, Jane. This may be exactly what her father says it is. Your neighbor may be taking a break."

"Maybe, but I don't think so. She and I were in the middle of figuring out what was happening to her. She was excited to think there was probably an external cause. She wouldn't just up and disappear without telling me."

"You know her that well, do you? This woman who's lived next door to you for what, ten months?"

"Then never mind about me. She was up for a partnership at her law firm. She wouldn't abandon her job. She wouldn't have missed an important meeting this morning."

"Again, you base your conclusion on your long and intimate knowledge."

She could hear the teasing in Alvarez's voice. "Based on my recent and deep association," she clarified.

"I stand corrected. Call me in the morning and let me know if she's back. If not, we'll go from there."

Harry looked up from the Red Sox game on the TV when she came into the room. "What did Alvarez think?"

"I can't tell. I wish he would take my client's disappearance more seriously. He still seems to believe she'll turn up from some spontaneous vacation. But he did agree to check with the security company."

"That's progress." Harry patted the seat next to him. When Jane sat down, he took her in his arms. "It will all be okay. You'll see."

Chapter Sixteen

In the morning, there was still no sign of Megan. Jane awoke to the smell of coffee and a text from Andy Bromfield.

Anything?

She texted back. **Nothing I can see from here. Will go over shortly.**

Let me know. Can't focus on work. I'll check in later.

As soon as she was dressed, Jane walked next door and rang Megan's doorbell. The house was silent. She knocked and rang the bell alternately for over a minute, reluctant to give up. Harry gave her a questioning look when she came back into the kitchen. She grabbed a cup of coffee and sat across from him.

She held the cup up. "Thank you." She wasn't ready to tell him the missing young woman lived next door. She loved that he didn't press her about where she'd been.

Alvarez called while they were eating breakfast. "Is she back?"

Jane excused herself, went to her office, and closed the door. "She's not answering her door if she is. I'm scared something is really wrong."

"I'll go over to Acme Security to see if I can charm them into giving me the logs."

"Thank you."

When Jane returned to the kitchen, Harry gave her a quick kiss and prepared to leave. "Try not to worry too much," he told her. "You won't succeed, but try."

Jane went out to her garden. The day was slightly cooler than the ones before it, but still it hadn't rained. It wasn't her day for watering, so she focused on breaking up the dirt so it would take the water better the next day. She cut a half-dozen flowers off the hydrangeas along her back fence to bring into the house before the blooms passed. She put them in a purple vase that had belonged to her mother and placed it on a table in her office. Through the windows, she caught sight of two people making their way down her garden walk. It was only then she remembered it was an office hours day.

"Yoo-hoo! It's me." Phyllis appeared around the corner of the house as soon as Jane opened the door. "I've brought company."

Behind Phyllis was an older man Jane recognized as a neighbor. He lived in a big white stucco house somewhere nearby, though Jane couldn't remember exactly where. She could picture him in his front yard, a rake in his hand, cleaning up the leaves that fell from a big maple, but she couldn't for the life of her picture the street.

"You know my neighbor Ralph Pilchner, don't you?" Phyllis stepped inside. The man, not so at home in Jane's house, stayed back.

Jane held out her hand. "Hello, Mr. Pilchner, I'm Jane. Please come in."

"I was walking Molly, and Ralph and I got to talking," Phyllis continued. "He needs help with a neighbor problem." Molly was Phyllis's young cocker spaniel. It was difficult to determine which of them was more excitable, or, as they came down the street, who was walking whom.

"Come, sit down." Jane gestured toward her guest chairs, and they sat. "How can I help you, Mr. Pilchner?"

"Call me Ralph."

"Ralph lives on Old Deer Path," Phyllis told Jane, "about halfway down. His backyard abuts mine."

"Of course," Jane said. Old Deer Path started across Birchwood Lane from Jane's and Megan's houses and ended in a cul-de-sac. There were only about a dozen houses on it total.

"It's about my neighbors," Ralph started. "They've been feeding our cat."

Jane didn't know what she'd expected, but Ralph's problem had a comfortable, familiar feel. It was much more typical of her cases than a young woman asking her to determine if she was sane.

"It started in July," Ralph continued. "They left food out on their deck. She'd go over there and eat and sit in the sun on their railing. We could see her from our house. I didn't think much of it. But now it's escalated. They're letting her into their house. She spends more time there than she does at ours. She doesn't turn up at home for days at a time. I don't know what they're feeding her, but she prefers it. It's alienation of affection, I say."

Jane was used to these kinds of situations between neighbors. Not alienation of the affection of a cat specifically, but disagreements that could be easily settled if the parties would talk to each other. "Have you spoken to your neighbors about this?"

"Many times. They promise to stop feeding her, but they keep right on doing it. My wife is heartbroken. We've had Roo—that's the cat's name—for more than ten years."

"You can help, can't you?" Phyllis asked.

"Yes, I can help. Sometime in the next couple of days, if you like, I'll visit your neighbors and tell them how distressing Roo's absence is for you and your wife."

"I would like that very much. Their name is Marshall, number ten. Thanks. What do I owe you?"

Jane named her hourly rate. Sometimes it was enough to encourage people to handle these situations on their own. But Ralph's face lit up with a relieved smile. "Thank you. Thank you so much."

Chapter Seventeen

Jane walked Ralph and Phyllis to the sidewalk and waved as they set off in opposite directions. She intended to return to her garden but instead stood staring at the brick front of Megan's house. The conversation about Ralph's cat had stirred up a worry that had lingered since the previous morning.

She pulled her cell phone out of the pocket of her skirt and called Andy Bromfield, whose name appeared many times in her list of recent calls.

"I'm concerned about Wembly," she said when he picked up.

"Me too," he answered. "But I'm more worried about Megan. I'm going crazy here. I feel as if I should be out nailing fliers to telephone poles."

"I don't think we need to go there yet." Jane's heart went out to the poor man. "But I would feel much better if I knew Megan had made arrangements for Wembly.

That would mean she left voluntarily. Do you know the name of her kennel?"

"That's the thing," Andy said. "I don't think she boarded Wembly, or at least never that I heard. She had a cat sitter."

"She did mention a cat sitter when she was listing people who had her alarm codes," Jane said. "You wouldn't know who it is?"

"No. Some kid from the neighborhood. That's all I know."

"Boy or a girl?"

"Girl, I think. But why? Wembly isn't at the house."

Jane hesitated. The day before they had been rushed and anxious. Maybe Andy had missed the cat. Maybe the two cops had as well. "The cat sitter might know where Wembly is, or at least know the name of his vet. Maybe we can track him down from there."

"Megan didn't go away on her own," Andy insisted.

Jane said she'd keep in touch and ended the call. Then she walked around the corner to Helen Graham's house.

"A teenage cat sitter, you say?" Helen led Jane out to the screened porch overlooking her normally lovely garden, which was now as thirsty and droopy as Jane's. Helen had poured iced tea, adding lemon and sugar to Jane's glass without asking. They'd been friends for a long time.

"Probably a girl." Jane hadn't said why she was looking for a cat sitter. Helen knew full well she didn't have a cat. She probably assumed Jane was working on a case—a case involving a cat, not a missing woman.

"Hmm." Helen looked at the ceiling, searching her memory. "This shouldn't be hard. Who has a teenaged girl?"

While the number of little kids in the neighborhood had dwindled to zero, there were teenagers living among them, children of the wave of double-income power couples who had preceded the foreign investors.

"The Brewers?" Jane said.

"Monica? She's in college out of state."

"The Singers?" Jane tried again. "Sarah's only ten, but she's a possibility."

"Unlikely. I can't see Wendy letting a ten-year-old go into an empty house alone." Wendy Singer was super diligent about her parenting, as she told anyone who would listen. "Maybe Wendy goes with Sarah," Helen suggested.

"All right," Jane said. "I'll put Sarah on the list. Maybe the Kolakowskis' daughter?"

Helen was indignant. "Would you let that girl anywhere near a beloved cat?"

"That's judgmental. Maybe Greta's a good kid who just happens to look as if she lives at a truck stop. I'm putting her down."

Helen snorted, a ladylike sort of a snort, and then thought again. "What about the Templetons?"

"The Templetons?"

"They live over on Dundee Street, but I see the girl—Charlotte, I'm pretty sure her name is—walking her dog by our house after school almost every day. I've chatted with her quite a few times."

Dundee Street was a quarter mile away, just outside their neighborhood, a broad boulevard instead of a winding lane. If this Templeton girl walked her dog on their street, she was obviously an animal lover. If Megan had seen her, it seemed entirely plausible she would have asked the teenager to look in on the cat.

"Thanks," Jane said. "Charlotte Templeton. Sarah Singer. Greta Kolakowski. I'll check them out."

When she got home, she called Sarah Singer's mother. They were neighbors, and Jane had Wendy's contact information in her phone, though she couldn't remember how she'd come by it. Wendy was an award-winning architect and would certainly be at work, but she might pick up her cell.

She answered on the first ring. No, Sarah did no pet sitting. She was allergic to cats in any event. Good luck finding someone.

Jane didn't set her straight. That would have opened a whole can of conversational worms.

Karen Kolakowski also answered her cell phone. She ran a busy restaurant on the other side of town, and Jane could hear the buzz of conversations and the clink of cutlery in the background.

"Cat sit? I don't think so. But Greta doesn't tell me half of what she does."

"This would be for someone in our neighborhood who would have given her access to her home to feed her pet."

"Access to an empty house? Great. Something new to worry about."

"I don't think Greta could use the house for parties or anything like that. The owner has cameras she can check from her phone."

"This gets worse and worse. But honestly, I don't think Greta works for your neighbor."

Jane thanked Karen for her time and clicked off.

She didn't know the Templetons at all. It was easy to find their address on the Internet but not a phone number. Jane would have to walk the short distance to their house

and ring the doorbell. It was one-thirty, too early for
school to be out, so Jane made a tuna sandwich and ate it
at the kitchen counter with her eye on the digital clock on
the microwave.

By three-thirty she'd talked to Andy Bromfield twice
and left a message for Alvarez that she hoped sounded
curious but not insane. She judged that wherever Charlotte Templeton went to school, she was probably home
by now.

Dundee was a busy street with a strip of brown grass
down its center. The houses that lined both sides were
large two-family dwellings, most of them well maintained. As she walked along, Jane kept her eye out for the
Templetons' number, fifty-seven. When she got there she
found a dark gray house with a deep front porch and a
heavy wooden door with a leaded glass window in it. The
Templeton name was above the bell for the first-floor
apartment.

The door was answered by a teenager with blue eyes
and long blond hair. She kept the locked screen door between them, as she must have been instructed to do by
her parents when she was younger. Her dog, some kind of
a collie-spaniel mix, sat in the hallway behind the girl,
waiting for a sign—friend or foe?

"Are you Charlotte Templeton?" Jane asked. The girl's
eyes widened. "Do you look after Megan Larsen's cat
when she's out of town?"

Charlotte blinked, and her eyes returned to their normal size. That Jane knew her name had been alarming,
but if Megan had sent her then she might be okay.

"I'm Jane Darrowfield, by the way."

Charlotte nodded and stepped out onto the porch. "I

cat sit for Wembly. Did Megan send you? Do you need a pet sitter?"

"I don't," Jane confessed. "I'm Megan's next-door neighbor."

"The stucco house or the stone one?"

"The stucco. I know this is going to sound like a weird question, but did Megan ask you to look in on Wembly this week? Did she mention anything about leaving town?"

Charlotte took a big step backward, away from Jane. "I thought you said you knew her."

"Megan isn't home, and I'm concerned about Wembly, so I wanted to know if she'd made an arrangement with you. It's a long shot really, because the cat doesn't appear to be in the house. Do you know of a kennel she would have used, or the name of Wembly's vet?"

"Don't assume that." Charlotte spoke quickly, her response automatic.

"Don't assume what?"

"Wembly doesn't like strangers. When I'd go in to feed him, he always used to hide. I had to look for him everywhere. He's not so shy with me anymore, but unless you've looked all over, you shouldn't assume Wembly isn't in the house." Charlotte paused, staring at Jane. "Is something wrong?"

"Not at all." Jane rushed to reassure her. "I'm just trying to track Megan down. I thought the cat might give me a clue."

"He's probably at her house," Charlotte insisted.

"Thank you," Jane said. "By the way, since you look after the cat, you must have the codes for the alarm system for Megan's house."

Charlotte nodded. "The garage door code, the inside door code, and the code to turn off the alarm."

"Do you have the app, the one that lets you turn off the alarm from your phone?"

"I have the numbers in my phone. Megan sent them to me as a text. But I don't have an app, no."

Chapter Eighteen

On her way home, Jane stood at the end of the walk and again stared at Megan's house. She called Andy, who surprised her by not picking up, and Alvarez, who surprised her because he did.

"Did you get the logs for the security system from Acme?" Jane asked.

"Hello to you too." Alvarez honored their joke. "I got one night's worth, last night, that's it, and only by telling the woman there I believed her client was in danger."

"You mean you got it by batting those long dark eyelashes at Agnes from Acme."

"I got it by using the persuasive skills I've learned as a law enforcement professional." He was in on the joke, not offended. "I got a buddy on the state police to look at what little I got."

"Did the log show anyone manipulating Megan's system?"

"No." Alvarez paused. "It's what the log didn't show. Someone entered or left the house via the door from the garage at six-twenty p.m."

"That was Megan, coming home from work."

"Someone entered or left at six-thirty via the front door."

"That was me," Jane said. "Megan called as soon as she got home, and I went over for our meeting."

"And someone entered or left via the front door at seven-seventeen."

"Me again, after we met."

"Ms. Larsen didn't leave with you?"

"Heavens no. I would have said."

"Because that's it. No one enters or leaves again until Andy Bromfield shows up at eight-thirty a.m."

"How can that be?"

"My buddy on the state police has three theories. One, the logging on Ms. Larsen's security system works sporadically. Acme probably checks only to make sure the logs are there, not that they're accurate."

"Agnes from Acme told me they constantly monitor the logs."

"A vendor lying about their service? I can't imagine." Alvarez ramped down the sarcasm. "My friend thinks this is the most likely explanation."

Jane wasn't buying it. "Or?"

"Or Mr. Bromfield is lying about what he found when he got to the house. He spent almost half an hour there before he called us."

Jane stood on the hot sidewalk, absorbing what Detective Alvarez had said. "But if he's the one who did something to Megan, why call you? Sure, someone would have figured out she was missing soon enough—her office, her father, her friends—but if he did something to her, he would have had hours more to cover his tracks if he hadn't called you." When Alvarez only grunted, Jane asked, "What's your friend's third theory?"

"That Ms. Larsen is still in the house."

Jane stared at the solid brick building. "Oh my goodness."

"Jane, she's not in the house. We searched it, remember?"

"Does this mean you'll open an investigation? You could come back and search again."

"The most likely explanation is the system logs are off somehow, but I admit I'm less comfortable than I was. My next call will be to Larsen to see what he wants to do."

They said their good-byes and ended the call. Jane looked at Megan's house. If Wembly was in there, caught in some corner or behind a closed door, he would be thirsty and starving by now. And what if Megan was trapped somewhere inside, unconscious?

"The heck with it," she said. "I'm going in."

Chapter Nineteen

Jane returned to her house and retrieved the piece of paper Megan had given her with the security codes on it. Then she went back to Megan's house and let herself in. She carefully typed the code into the keypad attached to the doorframe of the garage. The door slid noisily open. The garage seemed cavernous, especially because it was empty. Jane pressed a button, and the door slid down behind her.

Squinting at the paper, Jane punched four numbers into the keypad on the door that led from the garage to the kitchen. Once inside, she did the same with the keypad that disarmed the alarm.

Jane let out a long breath as she stood alone in Megan's white kitchen. "Here, kitty, kitty," she called. "Wembly!" Only the hum of the stainless-steel refrigerator echoed back.

Jane crept through the house. Wembly's food still sat in the bowl where Jane had poured it the day before. The half-full mug of tea was still on the coffee table. The crocheted throw was draped haphazardly on the back of the couch. Jane examined the afghan more closely. It was lumpy and old, black square frames with garishly colored centers, made of cheap, synthetic yarn. Jane didn't crochet, but she had friends who did, and she could tell the throw was made by a beginner, someone with little skill. She wondered if Megan had made it when she was a child.

The room was untouched. Megan had not been home.

Jane paused in front of the vision board in Megan's kitchen, studying it more carefully than she had on her previous visits. The collage was almost childish, the edges cut in imprecise waves and the layering haphazard. It was a testament to a person who loved babies, cats, and tropical islands. There were groups of kittens, all different colors, and proud grown cats. Similarly, there were groups of babies sitting and laughing and one big cutout, the one Jane had noticed the first day, of a seated baby with curly brown hair and brown eyes smiling right into the camera.

Jane looked carefully at the photos of tropical gardens and swaying palm trees with bright blue water behind them, hoping they would give a clue as to some favorite island resort Megan might have taken off to visit. But the photos were generic, taken from travel magazines. Jane couldn't discern anything unique about them.

Jane went into Megan's study. The white-walled room was bare-bones. The stagers had done little more than suggest an office, and Megan hadn't added any furniture to make it homier. As the police officer had reported, there was a laptop on the table that served as a desk, plugged in and open but turned off. There was no place for Wembly or anyone else to hide. Jane went back to the great room.

Calling for the cat, she climbed the stairs to the second floor. The carpet on the stairs and in the hallway was white. That would change when a child came into the house. If Megan ever came back. If she was successful in her attempt to adopt.

Jane opened the first door she came to. Inside was a guest room, also barely furnished. A queen-sized mattress sat on a metal frame. There were no bureaus, night tables, or bedside lamps. A few empty wooden hangers hung in the double-doored closet. The bed was not made up. It seemed doubtful Megan had many guests.

The guest bathroom was equally stark, all white subway tiles on the walls and black and white hexagonal tiles on the floor. Jane opened what she thought was a linen closet to make sure Wembly wasn't trapped inside and found a stacked washer and dryer. "Are you stuck?" she called to the back of the space. Silence.

When Jane opened the next door, her heart skipped a beat. Unlike every other room in the house, the walls were not white. They were painted a pale mint green, a color for babies, and there was a mural featuring Winnie the Pooh on the wall, his red shirt pulled up over his round tummy. The room wasn't furnished. Perhaps Megan didn't want to get too far ahead of herself. Or perhaps she'd begun the effort and then abandoned it when she began to doubt her mental health. "Wembly, Wembly!" Jane called. She waited and then closed the door, feeling as if she were closing it on Megan's dreams.

During the renovation, the master suite had been added over the double garage. A hallway divided the original bedroom that led to the addition. Clark Kinnon had used the old bedroom to create a large bathroom on one side and walk-in closet on the other. The new master bedroom was huge and, unlike the rest of the second floor, it looked lived-in. There were fabric shades on the windows and pictures on the walls. A king-sized bed was on the back wall facing the windows over the garden. Did the huge bed make Megan feel lonely? Jane shook her head. *Stop it, you're projecting. It would make you feel lonely. That's not the same thing.*

The portion of the bed nearer the door had been slept in. The cream-colored summer blanket and white top sheet were pulled back, revealing a long triangle of the bottom sheet. Megan had gone to bed before she left.

Midway between the bed and the doorframe, a single white mule-style slipper sat askew on the white rug. Jane stared at it. Neither the police officer nor Andy had remarked on this detail. It would be hard to tell a law enforcement professional that a single slipper in the middle of an otherwise tidy room meant anything. But the sight of it caused Jane's gut to churn. Her instinct was to pick it up, but she knew she shouldn't. If Megan didn't reappear, if Alvarez came around to Jane and Andy's way of thinking, the bedroom might be a crime scene and mucking about in it wasn't going to help matters. "Here, kitty, kitty, kitty," she called from the door.

There was no answering meow. Jane walked across the room, continuing to call. She stood by the side of the bed and carefully lowered herself to her knees to look under it. There was nothing, just an expanse of white carpet.

Grunting, Jane used the bed to lever herself up. She left the bedroom, walking carefully around the white mule, and went back downstairs.

Back in the kitchen, Jane noticed the basement door was open about six inches. She hadn't noticed a litter box during her search, and the basement seemed like a logical place for it. Jane wasn't averse to basements as a rule, though the basement of a house whose owner had inexplicably disappeared did give her pause. One of the uniformed officers had searched it, but he'd been looking for a woman and only tangentially for a cat.

Jane flicked on the light at the top of the stairs and trod carefully down the wooden steps. The basement was clean and dry and almost empty. It didn't smell of mildew or anything else, certainly not mold, but it did smell like a basement. Megan wouldn't have had much to store, coming from an apartment she'd shared with Ben. The new heating system took up barely any space, same with the efficient water heater. A plumbing chase came down one wall. The ceiling was high, high enough that the big open space could be converted for living, but for now it was simply a basement. Jane took her cell phone from her pocket and turned on the flashlight app, searching the dark corners for Wembly.

A light glowed from a wall under a portion of the kitchen, and Jane moved toward it, intrigued. It was some kind of a walk-in wine refrigerator with a light on inside. Jane opened the stainless-rimmed glass door. Apparently Megan wasn't a wine connoisseur. There were only three bottles on the tilted shelves, some papers and a slim cardboard box on another shelf. "Here, kitty, kitty." Jane took two of the bottles off the shelf and used them to prop open the door. The refrigerator must open from the inside, but Jane wasn't taking the chance of being trapped in an empty house.

"Here, Wembly." A light glowed dimly from the back wall. Jane moved toward it. As the space came into focus, she realized what she had taken to be the wall at the back of the refrigerator was actually a door. The wine shelves had concealed the frame. Jane reached for a handle, but there was none. "Wembly!" It came out of her mouth as a ragged cry. She wasn't calling for the cat. Her pulse raced. She banged on the door. "Come out," she pleaded.

Then she glanced up and to the right. A keypad and a camera. "A panic room," she said aloud. The logs had said Megan never left the house. Jane banged on the door as forcefully as she could. "It's Jane. I'll get help!"

Chapter Twenty

Jane took a breath to steady herself. All she could picture was Megan trapped inside. Megan the sleepwalker. Perhaps she was injured or unconscious, or was sitting in the dark, hungry and thirsty.

Jane reached up to the keypad and tried the garage door code, the kitchen door code, and the alarm code, hoping one of the numbers did double duty. On the third try the keypad glowed red, and Jane was fearful that another attempt would trigger some kind of lockout period, or worse.

There was no cell reception inside the wine refrigerator, and Jane stepped out gratefully, uncertain if she was shivering from the cold or from anxiety. She found the number for Cambridge Police headquarters and called.

"Is Detective Tony Alvarez available?"

"I'm sorry. He just left on a call away from the office.

Can I take a message or put you through to his voice mail?"

"Please get a message to him to call Jane Darrowfield right away."

"If this is an emergency, I can put you through to nine-one-one dispatch."

Jane stared at the phone. What to do? She considered calling 911, but how would she explain she was in her neighbor's house and was concerned that the woman, though not reported missing, had been locked in her panic room for almost two days?

"No, thank you. I'll wait for Detective Alvarez."

She had Alvarez's cell phone number. She'd been reluctant to use it in the past, but this felt like an emergency, if not an emergency she could explain to a 911 operator. If Megan had somehow shut herself in the panic room, was it stocked with water and food? Probably not. Megan wasn't a Russian oligarch or the child of a minor Saudi prince. The room had probably seemed as useful a part of the house as the wine refrigerator.

Jane called Alvarez's cell.

"Is she home?" That he picked up while he was out on a call told Jane he was concerned about Megan too.

"No. I'm in Megan's house. I've found a, I'm pretty sure it's a panic room in the basement. I'm worried she's inside."

"Stay there. I'll finish up here and meet you."

The call ended and Jane stared at the phone. There must be something she could do. She called another number.

"Acme Security."

"Hello, is this Agnes?"

"To whom am I speaking?"

"This is Jane Darrowfield. I spoke to you yesterday about purchasing a security system for 40 Birchwood Lane."

"How can I help you?" Agnes's tone was neutral, neither helpful nor annoyed.

"I'm next door at number forty-two, Megan Larsen's house. She has one of your systems." Jane paused. How to explain the situation for the greatest chance of results? "Ms. Larsen asked me to supervise some work here at the house, and I need to get access to the panic room. None of the codes she gave me seem to open it. Can you help?"

There was a long pause from the other end. "You, who are not the homeowner, are asking me to help you enter the safe room?"

It was time for the truth. "Megan is missing. I'm worried she may be inside."

Agnes sighed deeply. "You do understand that providing the code for a safe room to a total stranger, especially when the homeowner may be inside, is the exact opposite of our business model."

"I do, but this is an emergency."

"It is always an emergency. That is what safe rooms are for." But then Agnes relented. "Are you near the door to the safe room?"

Jane stepped back into the wine refrigerator, hoping she wouldn't lose the signal. "Yes."

"There's a small monitor mounted above the keypad. Do you see it? That should allow you to see if anyone is inside."

Jane looked at the monitor. The screen was black. She felt around to see if there was a way to turn it on. There was not. In fact, a button glowed, making it appear the monitor was already on.

"I think the monitor is on, but the screen is black," Jane reported to Agnes.

"That means the camera has been turned off. Your homeowner did that."

Because I told her to. "I'm not a total stranger." Jane gave it one last try. "I have authorized access to the house."

"Though not, apparently, to the safe room," Agnes responded.

"What can I do?" Jane hurried up the cellar stairs, hoping for better cell reception and for the sound of Alvarez's car pulling into the drive.

"Call the police. If they agree the door needs to be opened, they'll contact us, and I'll send a technician out."

"You can't open it from there?"

"We can do a lot of things from here—turn off alarms, notify authorities of a false alarm, even access the cameras or turn up a thermostat. Opening safe rooms, however, requires our presence on site. When the police arrive, have them call us."

Agnes disengaged, and Jane stared at the screen on her phone. As she looked, she got a text from Alvarez.

There in 20.

She called Clark Kinnon's office.

"Clark Kinnon Homes." Jane recognized Gloria Zinn's voice.

"Is he there, please."

"Mr. Kinnon? I'll find out. What is this in regard to?"

"It's Jane Darrowfield. I was there yesterday and spoke to him about my client Megan Larsen's home at

42 Birchwood Lane in Cambridge. I'm here at the house and I'd like to speak to him about the panic room."

Kinnon's voice came on the line. "What?" Gloria Zinn had transferred the call without saying a word.

"Hello, Mr. Kinnon. This is Jane Darrowfield. We met—"

"I know who you are." He inhaled, and his tone softened slightly. "How can I help you today?"

"Megan isn't available, and I need to get into the panic room at her house. I wonder if you have the original code from when it was installed."

"You're kidding."

"I wish I were, but it's a matter of some urgency to open the door."

"I don't have the code, and I wouldn't give it to you if I did. I suggest you contact Acme Security and the local police."

"I find it curious that in our discussion about the alarm system yesterday you didn't mention a panic room."

"I told you the type of clientele I expected when I developed the property. That should have made it clear there would be one." *Click.*

Chapter Twenty-one

Jane opened the front door as soon as she heard Alvarez pull into the driveway.

"Show me where it is," he said.

Jane guided him down the basement stairs and through the wine refrigerator to the panic room.

Alvarez examined the door. "I was mad the uniforms didn't find this, but now I get why they didn't." He turned to Jane. "Tell me again. Slowly. What makes you think Megan Larsen might be inside?"

Jane took a deep breath. "Megan is a type A personality, a high achiever. Her father says she sleepwalks when she's stressed. She's up for a big partnership at work and has been feeling as if she's being watched in her own home. I think we can agree either circumstance would be stressful." Jane paused and continued. "The combination would put anyone over the edge. Her bed was slept in the night she disappeared. There's a slipper sitting in the middle of her bedroom floor, as if it fell off when she was walking or running." Jane looked at the locked door. "What if she was sleepwalking and entered the panic room? What if she was awake and chasing the cat, who still hasn't turned up, by the way. What if she hurt herself in there? We're running out of time. Do you really want to take the chance?"

Alvarez looked at his phone and pressed the numbers for Acme Security. "Hello, this is Detective Tony Alvarez, Cambridge Police Department. To whom am I speaking?"

He nodded as Agnes spoke. "I'm at a property at 42 Birchwood Lane that I spoke to you about yesterday. Due to concerns about the well-being of the owner, we need you to open up the panic room."

Another pause. "I see. How long will that take?" Pause. "Great. Thank you. I'll look out for him."

"How long?" Jane asked when Alvarez clicked off.

"Fifteen minutes."

Chapter Twenty-two

Jane and Detective Alvarez waited upstairs in the living room. Neither could sit still. One sat on the white couch while the other wandered aimlessly through the kitchen and dining areas. As soon as that person sat down, the other one was up. At Jane's urging Alvarez went to Megan's bedroom to observe the errant slipper for himself. She heard him call Wembly as he walked through the second story.

At last there was the sound of another vehicle parking in the drive. Jane rushed to the door. "It's you." Jane took a breath to slow her heart rate.

Andy Bromfield hustled up the walk. "What's going on? I was driving past and I saw the detective's car."

Jane glanced at Alvarez, who shrugged. There was no reason not to tell. "I was looking for Wembly and discovered Megan has a panic room in the basement," Jane said. "I remembered what her dad said about sleepwalking and I got worried she was trapped in there. We're waiting for the technician from the security company to open it. It's a long shot," she admitted, "but we didn't want to take the risk of not opening the panic room once I found it."

"Of course, of course." Andy had grown paler throughout Jane's speech. "Why would Megan have a panic room?" His voice shook slightly. He obviously hadn't known about it.

"It came with the house," Jane told him.

"Mrs. Darrowfield tells me you've been calling Megan's friends," Alvarez said. "Did you learn anything?"

"Nothing. No one has any idea where she could be. Her friends are wondering what's going on. There's a lot of chatter. My calling around didn't help. And, of course, they've noticed at work. I've been using 'under the weather' and covering for her as best I can, but I don't think anyone's buying it. Megan would have to be at death's door not to be available on phone and e-mail." He blanched again when he realized what he'd said. "If this goes on any longer, I'm going to have to invent a dead grandmother."

"Does Megan have a grandmother or other close relation besides her father?" Alvarez asked.

"Not that I've ever heard."

"And you're sure she isn't with her mother?" Jane raised the possibility once more.

"Absolutely not."

"Do you know where her mother lives?" Alvarez asked.

"No idea. Megan never talks about her if she can avoid it."

The security technician finally arrived. He pulled his white van into the drive, squeezing behind Alvarez's and Andy's vehicles.

Alvarez met him at the door. "Detective Alvarez, Cambridge PD."

The technician had freckles and strawberry-blond hair that curled in wisps at the collar of his coveralls and a beard that matched the hair on his head. The name embroidered over his pocket read JUSTIN.

"Come this way." Alvarez led him down the stairs. Jane and Andy followed.

Justin looked at the panic room door and consulted an electronic device he held in his hand. "The camera's been turned off."

"Yes," Alvarez confirmed.

"I.D.?"

Alvarez produced his badge with a practiced flourish.

"As an officer of the Cambridge Police Department, are you asking me to open this safe room?"

"I am." Both of them spoke by rote. Each knew his part.

"Okay. Please stand outside this . . . whatever this is."

"Wine refrigerator," Jane said helpfully.

Justin went to work while the rest of them backed out of the tiny space. There was a beeping of the keypad and the sound of a heavy door swinging open. "Okay." Justin moved out of the way.

Andy dashed toward the entry, but Alvarez stiff-armed him out of the way and was the first one into the wine refrigerator. Jane brought up the rear.

"Meow." Wembly dashed around their legs and ran upstairs, presumably to his water bowl.

"Stay back." Alvarez shifted his position, and Jane could see into the dark room. There, lit by the thin strip of light coming from the wine refrigerator, in the middle of the floor, was one white mule-style slipper.

Chapter Twenty-three

Alvarez dismissed the security technician. "We'll take it from here."

Jane walked the man out. "Wait a second," Jane said to him. "You're Justin Vreeland, right? You came here in the late fall to teach the homeowner, Megan Larsen, how to use the security system."

Justin turned back from the front door to face her. His head swiveled, taking in the big room. "I thought this place looked familiar. I installed the system, too, but the house was just studs back then. But I was sure I'd been in this room after it was finished. It must have been when I came out to teach the lady who lives here how to use the system." He chuckled a little, looking at the mild disorder around the room. "The place was a mess then, too. Dishes in the sink, half-drunk mug of tea sitting on the coffee table, just like today. Is she okay?"

"That's what the detective is trying to determine. Do

you know if Ms. Larsen changed the alarm codes, or did she just use the same ones as the previous owner?"

"I don't know. I did teach her how to change the codes. That's standard in a training session, but I don't know if she actually did it."

"Is that something you can tell from your logs at the office?"

"Not easily. I'm guessing my office would want a warrant for the logs unless it was the homeowner who requested them."

"Thank you for your help today." Jane let him out, and a few moments later his van engine came to life and he backed out of the drive.

Alvarez and Andy came up the cellar stairs shortly after Justin Vreeland left. Jane refilled Wembly's water bowl while he begged with loud meows. "You have to see this means Megan was inside the panic room," she said.

She and Andy both trained their eyes on Alvarez, who didn't speak for a moment. "It is worrying," he admitted. "I'll touch base with my boss, and if he agrees I'll get in touch with Mr. Larsen to let him know we're moving Megan's apparent disappearance to an official missing persons status. Then I'll work with our press officer to let the media know we're looking for Ms. Larsen and we're concerned."

"You didn't call it a kidnapping," Jane said.

"I have no idea if it's a kidnapping. There's been no demand for ransom. No group or person has taken credit."

"Maybe she wasn't taken for money or publicity," Andy said. "Maybe someone took her to . . ." He faltered.

"I'm aware of what the circumstances might be," Alvarez reassured him. "I'll bring forensics in to see if we can determine if she was in the panic room recently."

"Maybe she was trying to get away from someone," Jane speculated. "She made it into the panic room but didn't get the door closed in time, and they snatched her."

"Or maybe the cat carried her slipper in there and somehow shut himself in." Alvarez offered his alternative version of events. "We'll see what we can find out. Both of you are free to go. I'll wait here for the team."

Andy left first, reluctantly, after eliciting promises from both of them that they would keep him informed.

"What can I do to help?" Jane asked Alvarez.

"Can you take the cat?"

"I don't see why not. Should I take him with me now?"

"No," Alvarez answered. "The crime scene techs may want to examine him. I'll bring him over when we're done."

He shut the door before Jane could ask, "Why would they examine the cat?"

Chapter Twenty-four

At home, Jane felt anxious and caged in. When the crime scene van pulled in next door, she couldn't take it anymore; she got in her car and drove to the pet superstore across the Charles River. She bought litter and a litter box, a feather on a string, and a rubber mouse. She tried to remember the brand of food Megan had in her cabinet but could not. The shelves of cat food ran half the length of the store, and none of the cans looked familiar. Jane bought a variety of the most expensive ones, figuring that would have to do. The total amount of the bill was heart-stopping.

While she was at the store, Helen and Phyllis both called. Neither left a message, but Phyllis also texted.

Police at Megan Larsen's. Weren't you just asking about her?

Jane didn't text her back. She wasn't ready to talk to anyone about what had happened. Harry hadn't planned to come over that night, and good listener that he was, as supportive as he was, Jane wasn't ready to talk even to him.

It was after eight o'clock by the time Alvarez came around the hedge with Wembly in his arms.

"If only he could talk," Jane said as Alvarez handed the big cat over.

Alvarez grunted. "It would make my job easier. What do you think about Bromfield?"

"I like Andy. He's a good friend to Megan." Jane studied Alvarez's expression. "You don't."

"He seems overinvolved. I can't believe he 'happened' to be driving by." Alvarez closed his eyes for a few seconds and then opened them. He was clearly exhausted.

Jane hesitated, not sure if she should add her speculation to the mix. "I think he's in love with her."

"That only makes him more dangerous." Alvarez looked over at his unmarked car, obviously anxious to leave and get on with the job.

They said their good-byes. Jane took Wembly into the house and set him down on the kitchen floor. She chose one of the cans of cat food she'd purchased and opened it, spilling the gooey, stinky contents into a bowl. Wembly sniffed it and turned his nose up. "It's okay, buddy," she told him. "She'll be back. Keep your strength up."

He turned his back to her and disappeared in the direction of her office. Maybe he didn't believe her. Jane had to admit he had a point. The lone slipper in the middle of the panic room floor, and its mate in Megan's bedroom, was deeply disturbing.

As was Alvarez's question to her at the front door. Why was she so sure that Andy was a good guy and a good friend to Megan? On the one hand, he was the one who had sounded the alarm that Megan was missing. As she had said to Alvarez, why would he have done that if he'd taken her?

But on the other hand, she had to admit Andy was around an awful lot. He said he'd been driving down Megan's street when he'd noticed Alvarez's unmarked car in the driveway. Why would an associate at a high-pressure law firm, being considered for a partnership, be driving around during the workday? The little street Jane and Megan lived on went nowhere. Andy was clearly checking out Megan's house. Why? And why lie about it?

What if Andy were the stalker, the gaslighter? He had Megan's alarm codes and phone app. Perhaps Megan had told Andy about Jane's theory about someone hacking the security system and it scared him. Maybe he thought taking Megan would end the investigation.

But he'd have to be pretty confused and crazed for that. Taking Megan would eventually have the opposite effect. The Cambridge PD would get involved and maybe the FBI. They'd have the warrants and whatnot and be able to look at more of the security system's logs. Things Jane could never do. Andy had seemed agitated and over-involved but not addled. He'd be thinking straighter than that.

What was Alvarez thinking? She should have asked him directly. But he'd wanted to get going, to get the formal investigation started, and Jane had wanted him to do the same. Whatever news the morning brought, they would be in a whole new phase.

Chapter Twenty-five

The news that Megan Larsen was missing hit the media like a bomb. She was pretty, white, successful, a Harvard Law graduate, the daughter of a prominent attorney, and residing in a big house in a fancy neighborhood. The news outlets lost their minds. The coverage was everywhere Jane turned. There were satellite trucks parked next door and reporters speaking earnestly into microphones with Megan's home as a backdrop.

Harry arrived unannounced at nine clutching his copy of the *Boston Globe* in a fist so tight it crumpled the paper. "You didn't tell me this woman who disappeared lived next door." He wasn't happy.

"I wanted to keep her identity confidential. It seems silly now. I keep expecting an announcement they've found her body."

Her voice was ragged as she said the last part, and

Harry took her in his arms. "I'm sorry. I know you liked her."

"She was thirty-four years old. She had her whole life ahead of her."

"Let's not start using the past tense yet."

Jane backed out of Harry's embrace and paced around the living room. "I want to do something. I want to help."

"The police are taking your client's disappearance seriously. It's what you hoped for. Let them do their job."

Jane nodded, miserable. "You're right of course. But I have this awful feeling I caused this."

"You didn't. I know it's hard advice to take with all the craziness going on next door, but try to go about your normal day. It will help, I promise." Harry looked at his watch. "I have a tennis game in an hour. I'll cancel."

"No. I'm fine. I'll take your advice. I do have another case." The problem of Roo the cat still awaited a solution.

He kissed her on the cheek, and then looked pointedly at the bowl of food sitting on the floor. "By the way, do you have a cat now?"

When Harry left after the explanation about Wembly, Jane opened a different brand of food and tried to entice the cat again. He turned up his nose at her latest effort. She left the food in his bowl in case he got hungry enough to change his mind. Then she gathered her phone and pocketbook and set off for the Marshalls' house.

She had to run a media gauntlet to cross her road. Two reporters attempted to interview her on her own front lawn. She put her head down and kept walking. The Marshalls were out on their front steps like everyone else in the neighborhood, staring up their street toward the cluster of satellite trucks and cars in front of Megan's house.

"Quite a fuss," Mr. Marshall commented after they'd

introduced themselves. He was Gordon, and she was Pam. They looked to be in their early seventies, both of them lean and fit, their faces tan.

"I wonder if I might come in," Jane said. "I have something of a delicate nature to discuss."

Gordon cocked an eyebrow at Pam, who raised her shoulders and let them fall, signaling "I have no idea what this is about." Aloud she said, "Of course, come inside."

They offered Jane coffee, and Gordon invited her into the living room at the front of the house, which was decorated in the jewel tones of the late nineties and looked comfortable and lived in. The morning's *Globe* was scattered on an ottoman.

Pam delivered the coffee on a tray, a cup for each of them. They looked at Jane expectantly.

She began, "I don't know if you know about me. I live on Birchwood Lane."

"Where all the TV trucks are," Gordon said.

"Next door. I have a little business, a postretirement business helping people out with problems that are vexing but not appropriate for the police."

Pam blinked rapidly. "I don't understand."

"Maybe it will help if I give you a concrete example. I was recently approached by your neighbor, Ralph Pilchner."

"Oh." Light dawned. Pam and Gordon gave knowing looks to each other.

Jane continued. "Ralph tells me you've been feeding the Pilchners' cat, Roo, for some time and have allowed her inside your home. He and his wife are quite disturbed, and they've asked me to talk to you about it."

Gordon sat forward in his chair, resting his elbows on

his knees. "I'm glad you've come about this. We've tried to talk to Ralph and Ceil about it, but it's clearly a difficult subject for them. Maybe you can help."

Jane took a sip of her coffee. "I gather this means you don't propose to solve the problem by not feeding the cat."

"It's not that simple," Gordon said.

"We used to be great neighbors." Pam's voice was high and breathy, like a young girl's. Jane had to strain to hear. "We've visited back and forth for decades. Our children grew up together. We're brokenhearted about the situation."

Brokenhearted. That was the term Ralph had used to describe his wife.

"I wonder if Ralph told you what's going on over there?" Gordon asked.

"No," Jane answered. "What's going on?"

"Our children were young together, and then they were gone. Ralph and Ceil seemed to settle in fine with it being just the two of them. That's when they got Roo," Pam said in her small voice. "But at the beginning of the summer, their son's marriage ended and he moved home."

"I'm sorry to hear that." Jane wasn't sure where the story was going.

"We were too," Pam said. "Though we had been at the wedding, and I can't say we were surprised."

"We were surprised it took so long," Gordon added.

"Anyway, the point is their son didn't move back alone. He moved back with three active kids, ages nine, seven, and five; a big German shepherd; and a cat of his own."

Jane began to see the bigger picture.

"That's when Roo started hanging out on our deck,"

Gordon said. "We tried to shoo her home, but she wasn't having it. I carried her over and left her on Ralph and Ceil's deck a bunch of times, but Roo was back here before I was."

"Eventually we did feed her," Pam admitted. "So she wouldn't starve. When it got so hot this summer, we started letting her inside."

"Ralph's come over a few times and taken her home, but she won't stay there," Gordon said. "We think what needs to happen is that the Pilchners have to recognize their household has changed and Roo is no longer comfortable over there. She's used to a quiet home. And they should let us keep the cat."

"Can you talk to them?" Pam asked. "Make them see how it is?"

Jane didn't respond right away. Her easy case had become more complex. "I'll tell them what you've said," she finally answered.

"*We've* told them," Gordon said. "But they can't hear it. They think we're catnappers. We're not. At least not on purpose."

"I'll see what I can do," Jane said, and that was that.

They finished their coffee and talked about the weather. By the end of August in New England the nights should have cooled, but that hadn't happened yet, deep as they were into September. And it still hadn't rained. Jane gave the Marshalls one of the cards Harry had printed for her that said JANE DARROWFIELD, PROFESSIONAL BUSYBODY, along with her e-mail address and cell number.

Gordon walked Jane out to the front steps. They both looked up Old Deer Path toward Jane's house. All the satellite trucks but one were gone, and a few cars remained.

"Scares you, doesn't it," Gordon said. "That something

might have happened to her right in that house. In our neighborhood."

"It does," Jane agreed.

"Did the police talk to you?" Gordon shielded his eyes against the morning sun.

"Yes."

"I've been wondering if I should call them myself. A big black SUV parks down at the end of the street." He pointed toward the end of the cul-de-sac. "During the day. For hours. Sometimes overnight, but mostly during the day."

"It doesn't belong to one of the houses down there?" They were in a part of Cambridge where every house had a driveway, so owners infrequently parked on the street. But it wouldn't be unheard of. A teenager or adult child with their own car, one too many to fit in the drive. Or a tenant in an auxiliary apartment. When Jane had first moved to the neighborhood, every other house had an apartment in the attic that was rented out to a grad student or couple. The kitchens and baths had been added in the housing crunch after World War II, and since the neighborhood was surrounded by universities, the apartments had continued to be a useful source of income for the homeowners. Now, with all the upscaling and remodeling, everyone had grown too rich to need the rent money and the apartments were mostly gone, but not entirely.

"It doesn't belong to anyone," Gordon said. "I got curious, so I asked around. Nobody on the street claims it."

"It's odd, I agree," Jane said gently. "When did you start seeing this SUV?"

"It's hard to know when I became aware of it," Gordon answered. "At first you think it's a one-time thing, or a guest or something. It was probably after Thanksgiving I really started noticing."

Jane looked up and down the little street. "When it parks there, which way does it face?"

"Toward Birchwood."

Megan's house would have been dead ahead through the front windshield. Alvarez had said that most people who went in for digital gaslighting were stalkers or abusers in the real world too. "Do you know the make?" she asked Gordon.

"Big and black. I'm not a car guy."

"Have you seen it recently?" Jane asked.

"Not for a couple of days."

"You didn't happen to copy down the license plate?"

"Nope. Now I'm sorry I didn't."

"You should call the Cambridge police and tell them." Jane wasn't sure how seriously he'd be taken without a make or license plate, but the police had to be looking for anything at this point. At least she hoped they were. "And if you don't mind, if you spot it again, could you call me?"

Chapter Twenty-six

Saturday turned to Sunday, which turned to Monday, and still there was no news. The story was still alive in the media. They used the same photo of Megan over and over.

Andy Bromfield texted Jane frequently, asking if she knew any more than the news reported. She could tell he wanted her to call Alvarez to fish for information, but she was using all her own willpower not to bother the detective. The last thing she wanted was to distract him from the search for Megan.

Wembly continued to turn up his nose at every brand of food she offered. Jane had opened nearly a dozen cans in a futile attempt to entice him to eat. "She'll be back soon," she reassured him, with more confidence than she felt.

The neighborhood was on edge. Each day stoked the collective imagination about what might have happened in Megan's house. Harry had stayed over every night, a comforting presence. Without mentioning it, he'd taken an old baseball bat out of Jonathan's room and put it under the bed.

The subject of Megan's disappearance was irresistible to everyone at the bridge game even though the group had thoroughly dissected it in multiple phone calls and a flurry of e-mails over the weekend.

"What I wonder is, why did she buy that house in the first place?" As Phyllis spoke she dealt the hand, punctuating each word with the thrust of a card toward a player's pile. "She didn't have a husband or kids. Why did she need all that room?"

"It's a publicity stunt," Irma said.

"I don't think that kind of publicity helps you get a partnership in a major Boston law firm." Helen spoke quietly, but the others had to acknowledge she was right.

"Then what?" Phyllis asked. "Was she really abducted right under our noses? Jane, you didn't hear a thing?"

"Neither me nor Harry." He and Jane were at an age where neither of them slept very well. She had trouble falling asleep, worrying over the events of the day—and the events of the past. Harry was more apt to wake in the night to use the bathroom. Sometimes he went right back to sleep, but other nights he roamed the house like a restless ghost. Jane had taken to calling him "The Night Watchman."

"I was going to say we slept like babies that night," Jane said. "But I've never understood that expression. Babies wake up every two hours."

"Starving and incontinent," Phyllis added. "Not something to aspire to. I dealt and pass."

"Three clubs." Irma looked at Jane. "You know more than you've said."

"You do," Phyllis agreed. "Spill it."

Jane tried to laugh the inquisition off. "My lips are sealed."

That didn't work. Now all three of them were staring at her. "Seriously, Jane, what do you know?" Phyllis pressed.

"Seriously," Jane answered, "I can't tell you what I know. Pass."

"You were working for her!" Phyllis guessed.

Jane wasn't going to lie. "A little bit. For a couple of days before she disappeared."

"Was she afraid it was going to happen?" Helen asked.

"Not specifically. I would have directed her to the police if that had been the case. Of course, now I wish I had."

"Four spades." Helen ended the bidding and looked directly at Jane. "I know you won't talk about the specifics of a case, but you owe Phyllis and me this. Are we safe in our own homes? We both live in sight of Megan's house, and Phyllis lives alone."

"I think so," Jane answered. "I didn't see Megan's disappearance coming, so I hesitate to say one hundred percent. But I believe what happened to Megan, whatever it was, was specific to Megan."

"Meaning?" Phyllis pressed.

"Either Megan was targeted, which seems most likely, or Megan took herself off, which seems less likely every day, but we can't dismiss it entirely. It's the better scenario for Megan, so I can't quite give it up."

Helen played the hand expertly, to no one's surprise. Helen didn't bluff. "I wonder," she said, "not so much why she bought that house but how she afforded it."

"She's a lawyer, a Harvard Law grad with a big deal firm," Irma pointed out.

"That's not enough. She must have other money from somewhere."

Helen was right. A decade earlier being on a partner track at a white-shoe law firm might have been enough to buy into the neighborhood, though even those ambitious young people had tended to come in pairs. In the ensuing years the prices had continued through the roof, and the buyers fit the profile Clark Kinnon had outlined. Even he hadn't expected a buyer like Megan.

"Her father is a big-deal lawyer," Jane said.

"But he's alive?" Helen asked.

It was a legitimate question. Though the police had given regular updates to a hungry press and public, no tearful family had appeared before the cameras. Was that something they did only with little kids? "He is. He could have given Megan the money or even the house as a gift," Jane said. It was hardly unheard of. In fact, it had been a common sort of practice in this neighborhood even back in the days when she and Francis had moved in. Not that either set of their parents had a dollar to spare.

"And her mother?" Helen prodded.

"Alive." Jane took the cards from her right and cut them to her left. Helen tapped them, and Jane dealt. "As much as I've been able to determine."

"They say these millennials go one way or the other. Either they're crazy ambitious, success-oriented strivers like Megan Larsen or they're uninterested in the extreme. There's even a movement to 'retire first,' spend your lazy years while you're young and healthy, put off that 'real job' as long as possible."

"Is that a choice, or something they're stuck with?"

Phyllis asked. They were treading on potentially dangerous ground. They had eight children between them— Helen three, Phyllis four, and Jane one. All of their kids had made different choices about how to pursue adulthood with quite varied results. Or at least so it appeared to the older generation. Jane, of course, knew next to nothing about Jonathan's choices, except for his choice not to communicate with her.

"For some it's a choice," Helen said. "Probably not so much for others."

They settled into the bidding and then turned to other topics, but Jane was left wondering: What drove the choices Megan had made and, more important, had she been happy with them?

Chapter Twenty-seven

After bridge, Jane went home to her quiet house. Harry wasn't coming over later that evening. He'd reluctantly agreed to a break in his nightly rounds as the watchman to spend Rosh Hashanah with his sons and their families as planned. On his dating profile he had listed himself as "casually Jewish," something else he shared with his late wife, Elda, but not with Jane.

Both Harry's boys and their families had been welcoming and generous to Jane. In the past year, they'd invited her into their homes and cheered alongside her at their kids' Little League games. Jane relished the family gatherings given her situation with Jonathan, though sometimes it crept up on her and made the pain of what she was missing more acute, not less so.

Jane had never thought much about being a grandmother. She'd never known either of her own. But now, when Phyllis or Helen reported gleefully on their grandchildren's adventures, it was all Jane could do to maintain a tight-lipped smile and dry eyes. Jonathan's terrible silence made her memories painful in retrospect, but more devastating was the loss of the hope of a shared future.

The irony that she was spending her retirement fixing other people's problems while this huge hole in her life went unaddressed wasn't lost on her, or on her bridge friends. They had all remarked on it in one way or another, though not unkindly.

Much as she enjoyed her time with Harry and his family, Jane also tried to give them time to themselves. He, his sons, and their families needed time together without her to be the family they had once been as much as they could without Elda. Jane might be part of the memories they were making now, but she was not a part of their past—and who knew what the future might hold?

Wembly came down the stairs from the second floor and stared at Jane dolefully. There was still a lump of the latest food choice in his bowl. He wasn't eating enough, the bare minimum to stay alive. Whether he was pining or simply boycotting Jane's food selections she did not know. He came over to rub a jowl on her leg. She bent down and ran a hand along his muscled length.

She wished she'd grabbed his own food for him when she'd been at Megan's. Jane went to the window and looked across the hedge. Megan's house was quiet, unnaturally so. There had been no police or press there all day. Jane found the piece of paper on which Megan had written the access codes, lifted a canvas shopping bag from the peg beside the back door, and went out.

The hedge meant she had to walk down her driveway, out to the sidewalk, and then up Megan's drive, where she felt terribly exposed. She wasn't sneaking, exactly, but she doubted the Cambridge police would want her over there. At Megan's garage door Jane hesitated. Had the police changed the codes once Megan's disappearance became official? But as soon as she entered the numbers and pressed the button, the door rumbled open.

At the kitchen door, Jane hesitated again. Surely, the cops would have changed the passcode. But when she entered the one Megan had given her, the door beeped and swung open. Once inside, Jane turned off the alarm and took a deep breath to slow her hammering heart.

The house was silent. There was no sound of air-conditioning. Even the big refrigerator was quiet. It was unnerving. Someone had tidied. The half-drunk mug of tea was gone from the coffee table. Perhaps the crime scene techs had taken it to analyze? The crocheted afghan was missing from the back of the white leather couch. What had they needed that for? Jane doubted the police left every place they visited so spotless. But was the house a crime scene? Even the panic room had shown no signs of a crime. There was no body, no blood spatter, no weapon. What had the crime scene techs found?

Jane opened the lower cabinet next to Wembly's bowls, pulled out two six-packs of tiny cans of cat food and put them in her canvas shopping bag. That would keep him going for a while, and now that she had the brand name she could order more. After thinking about it, she also picked up his bowls, rinsed them in the sink, and put them in the bag. Perhaps that was the problem—unfamiliar dishes. When Alvarez asked her to take the cat, she had never considered how long she would have him. Perhaps Wembly was hers forever.

Jane turned to leave. The house felt creepier than it ever had, though for the life of her she couldn't think why. Megan's vision board caught her eye. Jane stepped forward to examine it. Really look at it. For the first time she realized what it *didn't* show. There were no photos of sleek corner offices, of lawyers pleading before judges, or lawyers doing anything at all. There were no photos of suburban houses, playrooms, children's rooms, anything a hopeful parent might keep. What did that mean?

Jane left quickly, pulling the kitchen door closed behind her. She went out through the garage door, put the code in to close it, and waited until it hit the concrete threshold with a *thunk*. Swinging the canvas bag, she hurried down the drive.

For the first time she seriously wondered whether Megan had engineered her own disappearance. She was up for a partnership at one of the most prestigious law firms in Boston, but her vision of herself in the future apparently didn't include being a lawyer. Or living in a house like the one she owned. Jane considered what Andy had told her about Megan. Had her successful father put her on a track she didn't know how to get off? That might be a reason to walk away.

Jane let herself in her back door. She emptied the generic food, obviously meant for lesser cats, from the unacceptable bowl and then opened the can she'd brought from Megan's. Wembly rubbed against her legs, meowing urgently.

"It's coming, it's coming," Jane assured him. She dumped the full contents of the can into his personal bowl. She wasn't sure how much he should eat, but the cat was plainly hungry. Wembly lunged for the food when she set it down, oblivious to anything else in the world.

Jane poured a glass of wine and went to the living

room. The days were growing shorter, the low sun of early evening casting long shadows on the rug.

Could Megan have engineered her own disappearance?

Was hiring Jane and planting the seeds of a creepy Internet gaslighter a part of the plan? Jane had never seen the lights flash, the thermostat creep up, the clocks jump forward. She had taken Megan's word for what was happening.

The law enforcement agencies searching for Megan would be going through more of the home security system logs. They would know soon if anyone had hacked her system.

But even as Jane worried about Megan's role in her disappearance, her mind argued against it. Megan was an adult. She'd extricated herself from her romance with Ben. She'd cut things off with her mother. If she wanted to leave Bookerman, Digby, and Eade she would do so. Despite her father's information about her nervous disposition, despite Megan's own voiced fears about her sanity, Jane had found her to be a mature, rational adult human.

Perhaps it was more pleasant to think about Megan on a tropical island somewhere, adopting a baby and a couple of cats and living a quiet, small life. More pleasant than thinking about what was probably happening. Megan dead, her body in a landfill or deep in the woods. Or being held captive by a madman.

Wembly, finished with his dinner, pranced into the room, purring happily. He looked up at Jane with anticipation and then jumped into her lap. A first.

Chapter Twenty-eight

Jane had dozed off in her chair, the reassuring bulk of Wembly in her lap, when her cell phone buzzed. Alvarez.

"Nothing going on next door?" he asked.

"All quiet," Jane said, leaving out the part where she'd been the one to disturb it. "The camera trucks are gone. What's happening with the case?"

Sometimes on previous cases he would tell her, and he did now. "Your neighbor has disappeared into thin air."

"I'm sorry I told her to turn off the cameras."

"The cameras would have helped," Alvarez admitted. "We are taking your lead seriously. We have specialists from the state police combing through the logs from Ms. Larsen's home security system to see if she was hacked."

"So you agree the two things must be related. Whoever was harassing Megan must be the one who took her."

"I'm not willing to say 'must,'" Alvarez responded, "but to have one person harass you and a different unrelated person abduct you would be terrible bad luck."

"You said yourself these digital gaslighters usually engage in other forms of abuse."

"It's a ways from harassment to abduction, though certainly not unheard of."

"Who's on your suspect list?" Jane asked. Nothing ventured, nothing gained.

"You know I can't tell you that," Alvarez answered. "I'd rather hear who was on yours."

Jane sat back in her easy chair, grateful to be asked. At least that way she was helping, maybe, a little bit. "I hadn't got very far. To manipulate the time, the temperature, the lights, and so on, it was someone who had the cell phone app and the correct codes."

"We know Megan gave the code for the app to Andy Bromfield," Alvarez said.

"And to her dad," Jane added. "And to me."

"It's usually the ex," Alvarez added. "What did you think of him?"

"Ben Fox. He seems like a nice guy," Jane answered. "Very concerned about Megan. Maybe not entirely over her."

"Do you think that's important, the 'not entirely over her' part?"

"Maybe. Could be." Jane was feeling cautious, not wanting to jump to conclusions. "I don't know. He didn't seem like the type."

"You'd be amazed who's the type." Alvarez's voice was sharp and sad and weary with all the stuff he saw in his job, stuff Jane normally didn't have to see.

"I'm sure I would be."

Despite his job, Alvarez wasn't usually so downbeat. His frustration and exhaustion had broken through, a rare instance of his letting his guard down. Perhaps he was trusting her more.

"There's also Clark Kinnon, who sold Megan the house in November," Jane continued. "He admitted to me that he had the codes and the phone app from when he renovated the house. I've talked to Kinnon a couple of times."

"I know who he is. What did you think of him?"

"I don't like him. But maybe that's because he's generally unlikeable."

Alvarez laughed a short tired laugh. "Anyone else?"

"There's one other person. Megan had a date a few months ago, a guy she connected with online. They met at Peet's for coffee. It didn't go anywhere after that. I met him. He's kind of creepy. But what strikes me particularly is what he does for a living. He's in computer security."

"Interesting," Alvarez admitted.

Jane felt a little thrill of victory. She gave him Howard Borg's contact information. "Did you ever find Megan's mother?" Part of her still hoped against hope that Megan was somewhere with her absent mom. Not the realistic part of her, but a more hopeful part.

"Not a word. Larsen claims he doesn't know how to reach her. She's an alcoholic who's bounced in and out of their lives for years."

"That's what Andy told me, too. Did Larsen say what name she uses? I mean, when they divorced did she keep his name or go back to her maiden name? Did she ever remarry?"

"Larsen said, and this is a quote, 'I have no idea what

she calls herself. Last I heard, she was selling scented candles at some store in western Mass.'"

"And with all those great clues, you couldn't find her?"

Alvarez chuckled, but when he spoke his voice was serious. "What concerns me more is that this case has been in the headlines every day. It's led the news. It's all over social media. Don't you think that if Megan's mother were in Massachusetts, even at the other end of the state, she would have contacted us by now?"

Jane felt the faint hope she'd been clinging to—the hope that Megan was with her mother—escape her body like a slow leak from a balloon. "You don't think Megan's mother's missing too?"

Alvarez paused. "I don't think she'd been abducted, if that's what you're asking. I think she's missing in action. Indifferent to her child who is in grave danger."

"Or dead," Jane said. "Her child who could be dead."

"Or dead," Alvarez confirmed.

Chapter Twenty-nine

Jane clicked off the phone, feeling the tension of the conversation in her shoulders. She and Jonathan had been estranged for more than a decade. The breach had come at his insistence. "Mother," he had said in their final conversation, "I need to take time off."

"From what?" Jane had been genuinely puzzled. Since Jonathan had graduated from Harvard, the school where he was a legacy and where his father still taught, he'd been indifferently and sporadically employed in a number of technology ventures, not one of which did anything Jane could understand. Or at least she hadn't been able to understand how any of them would result in a profit.

"From you," Jonathan had answered brutally and, as it turned out, finally. He had packed his books and clothes into a giant duffle bag and left the house.

Jane hadn't been too concerned. She'd assumed he'd gone to his father's house, which was less than a mile away, a frequent pattern during his stormy teenage years. Goodness knew he didn't have the funds to go anywhere else. Francis's second wife, his former department secretary, was at best an indifferent stepmother and occasionally a hostile one. Jane thought Jonathan would soon be back in his boyhood bedroom.

But when, after three days of silence, she'd checked with Francis, he told her he'd given Jonathan a thousand dollars and a car he'd been about to trade in to "see some of the country." Receiving this news, Jane had taken several deep breaths to calm herself. Jonathan was of age— more than—and there was no longer a custody agreement to govern what she and Francis were obligated to communicate to each other. Still, it would have been nice . . .

A little travel might be good for Jonathan. He hadn't been making much progress staying at home.

Jane left a cell phone message. Jonathan was still on her calling plan. Over the ensuing weeks and months, she left several more. Some of them teary and pleading, others angry and curt.

Jonathan was in touch with Francis, who assured her their son was fine, traveling westward, having the kinds of adventures people should have when they were young.

"Even though he lived in a dorm, remember he went to college less than a mile from his mommy," Francis said, using words chosen to prick her. Jonathan had never called her Mommy. "Let him sow his wild oats."

So Jane had backed off, stepping down the number of calls, the "I just want to know you're okay" texts and e-mails. And that had been the end. Two years later, she was notified that Jonathan had given up his cell phone number and plan.

That same day, Jonathan had deleted his Facebook. Jane missed it terribly. He hadn't posted anything since he'd left home, but in the sleepless, early morning hours Jane had often studied it, taking comfort in the photos from his high school prom and camping trips, even the drunken college parties. Since then, Jane had searched every social media site she could think of under every variation of Jonathan's name she could think of but had found nothing.

She turned to her photo albums and stared at images of the times they had spent together, the vacations in Maine, apple-picking in the fall, and New Year's Eves with the bridge club kids playing games. The photos of happy times together became fewer and further between in his teenage years, but that was normal, wasn't it?

Francis refused to pass messages or disclose anything he might know about Jonathan's life, wherever he was. "This is between the two of you." Jane suspected he didn't know much. Francis's main preoccupation was himself, which had always been an issue with his parenting. Knowing more than Jane did about Jonathan made Francis feel superior. Knowing what Jonathan was actually up to was probably a great deal less satisfying.

Finally, Francis had passed on the information that Jonathan had settled in San Francisco and had a good job in tech. The summer before this one, Jane and Harry had traveled to San Francisco so Harry could teach a class at a conference there. Harry used his connections to turn up a physical address for Jonathan. Jane had gone by Jonathan's house on a Saturday and had rung the bell. No answer. She had left a note saying she would be in the coffee shop on the corner and had waited for six hours, and returned, and left another note the next day and sat in the café again—except when she was so anxious she needed to move. She passed in front of Jonathan's house so often, she was worried a neighbor would call the cops. In the café, she studied the face of every appropriately aged male. Did Jonathan lurk under one of those full beards? But all the men were all too tall or short, broad-shouldered or fine-boned, different coloring, different ethnicity. None of them were Jonathan. She would know her own child.

Jonathan's house in a fully gentrified neighborhood offered no clues. It was painted wood, three stories, the front door up a steep set of steps like all the others in its row. But inside, was it one house—a place for a family? Or was it three lovely floor-though apartments lived in by single adults or couples? Or was it a bunch of single rooms, a remnant of the old, ungentrified neighborhood, lived in by young people who hadn't yet gotten a toehold in this expensive city? A decade was a long time, especially for the young. There was no telling what Jonathan's life was like.

Thinking about her son focused Jane on Megan's absent mother. Though Jane hadn't seen or heard from her son in over ten years, he lived on in her imagination. He got up every morning and went to a job he loved. She pictured a shadowy presence by his side who might be a wife or a girlfriend. It frustrated Jane that she couldn't get a look at her even in her mind's eye. And sometimes the indistinct person carried something that might be a child.

The point was, somewhere, Jonathan was alive and functioning in the world. Maybe he was even happy. It was Jane's most fervent hope.

If he had been missing, Jane would have wanted to know. If he had been in grave danger, she would have wanted to know. If he were . . . She stopped thinking about it abruptly. Somewhere, Megan's mother was living that nightmare and didn't even know it.

Chapter Thirty

Jane went to her office and opened her laptop. Detective Alvarez had access to information in state databases. He would know if Megan's mother had ever been arrested, or if she'd registered a car, maybe even if she had a bank account. He had Megan's laptop and phone, which would show whether she and her mother were in touch. He'd come up empty.

As a professional busybody, Jane had invested in other things like access to newspaper archives and genealogy sites. Not that Alvarez didn't have those, but Jane doubted the police had gotten that far yet. Megan's mother wasn't the object of their search.

Megan was nearly thirty-five. Counting backward, Jane guessed her parents must have been married between thirty-five and forty-five years ago. Edwin Larsen appeared to be close in age to Jane. The wedding announcement of a young lawyer who worked at a big-name firm in the 1970s or '80s would have been in the newspaper. Jane searched first in the digital archives of New England's paper of record, the *Boston Globe*.

It didn't take long to find the wedding announcement. Edwin Larsen and Laura Reeve had been married only a year before Megan was born. Larsen was not yet a partner at Franklin and Franklin, as the firm was called then, but he was described with the kind of breathless prose that marked an up-and-comer. In the photo that accompanied the article, he was handsome then as now, posture straighter and no potbelly, and he wore a triumphant smile. Laura looked uncannily like her daughter, or more accurately the other way around. A woman with the same long dark hair, pointed nose, and large mouth stared out from the photograph. She wasn't smiling.

Laura came from western Massachusetts—Stockbridge, the article reported. Had she returned to her hometown after her marriage ended? Perhaps she still had family out there who were in touch.

Jane quickly searched for Laura in the rest of the *Globe* archives, under both Reeve and Larsen. Edwin Larsen appeared frequently in the society columns and in stories about his cases. He seemed to specialize in working with major developers, the same field of law as his daughter. In the last few years Megan had made several appearances in the paper and then there was the riot of information about her since she'd gone missing. Laura didn't appear in a single article except the one about her wedding.

Jane searched for people with the surname Reeve around Stockbridge. There was one, Richard, who seemed to be the right age to be a brother. He owned a glass shop right in town. Jane made a note for later and kept moving in wider circles.

In the Berkshires, the mansions and grand hotels built for wealthy New York families at the turn of the previous century had turned into private schools, yoga institutes, religious retreats, and, yes, several rehabilitation facilities, most of them private. Jane wondered if any of them were the ones Laura had passed through during her attempts at sobriety. They would protect their patients' privacy zealously. No point in calling them.

At last, Jane sat back wearily, her eyes strained and dry. Random searches for Reeve in western Massachusetts had got her no further than Richard. It was late in the day but with any luck the glass shop would still be open. Jane picked up her cell phone and dialed.

"Gallery of Glass, Maggie speaking."

Jane's heart fluttered. Was it possible? "Megan?"

"No, Maggie." The young woman's voice turned suddenly cold. "Who's this?"

Jane doubled back. "I'm sorry. I thought you were someone else. I'm Jane Darrowfield, calling from Cambridge, Massachusetts, and you are Maggie—" Jane left the last part dangling in the air.

"Maggie Reeve," the woman responded.

The voice was too young to be the wife of Richard Reeve, unless he had married someone much, much younger. "Are you Richard Reeve's daughter?" Jane asked. "Is he available?"

There was a long silence. "My father doesn't work here anymore. He has…" There was a long hesitation. "He has memory issues. I'm sorry to tell you if you're a friend of his."

"I'm not," Jane clarified. "Though I'm very sorry to hear it." She cleared her throat. "I was looking for your father because I'm searching for a woman named Laura Reeve or Laura Larsen. I wonder, do you know her?"

This time the silence from the other end lasted even longer. Jane began to wonder if Maggie had put down the phone and walked away.

"What is this in regard to?" When she finally spoke, her tone was undisguisedly hostile.

Jane chose her words carefully. She sensed she'd only get one shot. "It's about Laura's daughter, Megan Larsen. You may have heard, she's missing."

"If you're a reporter, hang up right now."

"No!" Jane shouted at her cell phone. "I'm not. I'm Megan Larsen's next-door neighbor." She took a ragged breath and brought her voice down. "I'm a mother, too. A mother who's estranged from her child. And I know that if my child were in trouble, I would want to know about it. Is Laura your aunt? If you can confirm she knows Megan is missing, I won't trouble you any further."

"Laura is my father's sister." Maggie's voice was tight. "The situation here is not so simple."

"Please," Jane said. "Take my number. Just in case she has any questions or wants to talk."

Maggie agreed, and Jane rattled off the numbers, not even sure if the young woman was writing them down.

Chapter Thirty-one

In the morning, Jane put on a nice pink blouse, a navy-blue cotton skirt, and a pair of navy flats. She added a string of pearls, making her more dressed up than she usually was in her retirement, even when she was working on a case. She was headed downtown to a fancy law firm and wanted a look that would ease the way.

Jane had no idea if Edwin Larsen would be at his firm, but an office seemed like a better setting for a surprise visit than his home. She hadn't called ahead, fearing he would put her off, downplaying Megan's abduction as he had at the house six days earlier. There had still been no public plea from him for Megan's safe return. He must either truly believe Megan had gone off on her own or be in deep denial.

The receptionist at Franklin and Larsen scowled when Jane admitted she didn't have an appointment but then picked up the handset and dialed through to Edwin Larsen's executive assistant.

"I have a Ms. Darrowfield here for Mr. Larsen." (Pause) "No, she doesn't have an appointment. She came hoping he had a moment free." (Pause) "Yes, I'm aware he's very busy, and I'm sure Ms. Darrowfield is too. Perhaps you would simply ask him if he has time for her." This time the receptionist looked up at Jane and rolled her eyes. "Thank you," she said into the handset and hung up. She gestured toward a couch in the waiting area. "Ms. Brighton will be right out."

Jane preferred to stand, but she moved away from the front desk so she wasn't hovering. Larsen's assistant took her sweet time. Eventually she showed up, in a severe black sheath and skillfully made up. Dressed to intimidate.

"I'm sorry. Mr. Larsen has a busy schedule today. Perhaps if you had called and made an appointment." Her voice echoed around the cavernous reception area, loud and scolding.

"Perhaps he can spare a few minutes. It's about his daughter, Megan."

Ms. Brighton's haughtiness morphed into hostility. "If you are a reporter you will leave these premises immediately or I will call security."

"I'm not a reporter." Jane would not be pushed around. She had decades of experience dealing with these sorts of gatekeepers. She kept her voice low so the conversation was as private as possible given the receptionist sitting twenty feet away. "But I do know many reporters, and if Mr. Larsen doesn't agree to see me, I will call one and offer them an exclusive story about how he downplayed his daughter's disappearance to the police and delayed the search for her by thirty-six hours."

Ms. Brighton's dark eyes darted around the lobby, which was still empty except for the receptionist. "Come this way." She led Jane down a long hallway toward a corner office.

Jane stood outside the office while Ms. Brighton entered. Edwin Larsen shook his head. Vehemently. Jane read his lips. "Absolutely not."

Ms. Brighton bent toward him, whispering rapidly.

"Okay," he relented, so loudly this time Jane could hear him. "Bring her in."

"Mr. Larsen has a few minutes for you."

Jane entered as Ms. Brighton withdrew, throwing Jane an angry glance as she passed.

Larsen's office was fit for a named partner. The walls were dark wood and the desk acres of mahogany. Larsen stood when Jane entered and offered his hand. "Mrs. Darrowfield, we meet again." Unlike the denizens of Bookerman, Digby, and Eade or Ronson, Berriman, and Shoemaker, he was dressed in a suit, a navy blue, pin-striped one, complemented by a white shirt, silver cuff links, and a striped red-and-blue tie.

"Jane, please."

"And I am Edwin." He gestured to a couch against the wall miles from his desk. After Jane was seated, he took one of the tall-backed side chairs opposite. "I apologize, but I only have a few minutes. I'm due in a meeting."

"I understand." Jane settled onto the couch, which was covered in a gorgeous maroon leather but was too stiff to be comfortable. "Thank you for seeing me." She almost added "so graciously," but there was no point in sarcasm.

She gathered her thoughts for a moment while Larsen stared expectantly. "As you will have guessed, I've come about Megan. I'm so concerned about her. I wonder if the police shared anything with you that they haven't made public."

Larsen shook his head slightly. "They're sharing far too much with the public, in my opinion. I still believe Megan's absence is voluntary."

"The police no longer believe that after they found her cat and slipper in the panic room."

"I understand their concerns, but that is exactly the kind of thing Megan would do when she was under stress. Sleepwalk into the panic room, wake up, freak out, accidentally shut the cat in, run off to hide until she could get herself together."

"You seem certain."

"It's a pattern I've seen before. Not just in Megan, but"—he cleared his throat—"in her mother."

"Have you and Megan's mother talked about what's happening?"

"We haven't talked in decades. Laura is . . . not stable. She hasn't contacted me or the authorities since Megan's name has been splashed all around the news. That means she doesn't know Megan's 'missing,' she can't respond, or she doesn't care. I'm in no position to say which of those three is the reason."

"But you haven't reached out to her."

"I wouldn't know where to begin."

"Do you support Megan financially?" It was a direct question, perhaps even a rude one. Jane softened her tone, hoping to take the edge off the topic. "Her house was expensive, beyond what one would expect an associate in a law firm could pay."

Larsen's eyebrows flew up. "What are you implying? That Megan was into something illegal, something that got her abducted or killed?" Each sibilant *something* was accompanied by a tiny bit of spittle.

"Nothing like that," Jane rushed to say. "It's just that it's an odd choice for a young single woman, a big house in a suburbanish neighborhood. I keep wondering why she chose it and how she afforded it."

"Have you shared these 'wonderings' with the police?" Larsen demanded. Then before Jane could speak he added, "Not that it's the tiniest bit of your business, but Megan's grandfather—her mother's father—left Megan a considerable trust. She doesn't fully come into the money until she's thirty-five, but she's been able to draw from it since she was eighteen for specific reasons—education, the purchase of a home, and so on. She used some of the money from the trust to buy the house on Birchwood Lane."

It must have been a considerable trust to fund the cash purchase of such an expensive house and still have money left over. Did it mean anything that Megan was not simply well-off but rich?

"And now, if you'll excuse me." Larsen stood. His long legs and round tummy made him seem like a stork in a suit.

They said their good-byes. As Ms. Brighton walked Jane back down the long hallway, the firm was eerily quiet. There were no phone conversations to be heard through the open doorways, no visiting from one office to another, no clatter of keyboards from the admins' desks. When she peeked into the one office with an open door, the desk and bookshelves were empty, the space clearly unoccupied.

"How many people work here?" she asked Ms. Brighton.

"So many," Ms. Brighton answered. "You wouldn't believe it."

Out on the sidewalk, the city bustled, cars honked, and bicycle messengers wove in and out of traffic both vehicular and pedestrian.

Jane stood for a moment, thinking about Edwin Larsen and Megan. If Megan's money came from her mother's family, that left even more unanswered questions. Jane walked quickly in the direction of the Red Line, more determined than ever to talk to Laura Reeve.

Chapter Thirty-two

Jane pulled the orange Volvo she called Old Reliable out of her driveway and made her way to the Mass Turnpike entrance in Brighton. It would be a long trip to Stockbridge, practically at the other end of the state. Jane settled back to enjoy the ride.

The Berkshires in general, and Stockbridge in particular, were favorites of hers. Phyllis's daughter had a summer house in Lenox, near Tanglewood, where the Boston Symphony Orchestra spent its summers. The bridge club had borrowed it for extended weekends they called retreats, but which tended to be more boisterous than contemplative. Jane loved their visits to the Norman Rockwell Museum and to Edith Wharton's brilliant house, The Mount; drinks on the porch of the Red Lion Inn; and picnics on the lawn at Tanglewood.

The symphony season was over, but it still felt like summer as Jane made the turn onto Main Street in Stockbridge. Soon the leaves would be red and gold, the summer visitors replaced with the leaf peepers. The crowds were healthy, and Jane drove slowly, searching for a parking space. Finally she spotted one, about two blocks beyond her target, and pulled in.

Jane walked quickly, head down, to the Gallery of Glass, intent on her mission. But when she stepped through the door, the tinkling of a bell broke her concentration and she looked up and around.

In her many trips to Stockbridge, Jane had never been in the shop before. To the extent that she'd pictured it, which wasn't much, she'd anticipated a store full of souvenirs, maybe some vases, dusty and dank. Instead the space was huge, with white walls leading two stories to a skylight. Enormous glass sculptures were everywhere resting on stands or secured to the walls. The colors dazzled, and the pieces danced and swayed even when they stood still. In addition to the glass pieces there were knitted scarves, shawls, and throws draped throughout the shop. Jane reached out to touch one. It was a beautiful rich Mediterranean blue shot through with green fibers, made from delicate wool with tiny regular stitches. The soft goods contrasted with and heightened the beauty of the glass. "Oh, my." It came out of her mouth as she thought it.

"May I help you?"

The young woman behind the counter was slim and angular. Waves of brown hair cascaded down her back, and her sleeveless top showed off her tattoos. She couldn't have looked less like a real estate attorney, and yet Jane caught a glimpse of Megan in her wide mouth.

"I'm Jane Darrowfield. I called yesterday. Are you Maggie Reeve?"

"Oh." The well-practiced customer-is-always-right smile disappeared.

"I've come to see your aunt." Jane didn't leave room for argument.

The tanned brow creased over her hazel eyes. She chewed her lower lip, not obsessively, but once, and then drew a long breath. "My aunt, she's good. She's doing really well, sober for three years now. It's the longest she's ever achieved." Maggie paused. "But she's fragile, or at least we treat her like she is. My dad was the one who looked after her for years, confronted her when it was time to go back to rehab, picked her up when she was released. But my dad's not up to being her surrogate parent anymore and I'm left . . . not knowing what to do."

Jane reached across the counter and put a hand on the young woman's slender arm. She felt bone through the sheaf of muscle. "Perhaps you've got some tea, in the back?"

Maggie nodded and led Jane through a curtain behind the counter into a small but pleasantly furnished kitchenette office. She turned on an electric kettle and got two glass mugs down off a shelf, evidently taking Jane's suggestion literally. Jane approved. The poor young woman was stressed, and tea was exactly what was needed.

Jane watched as Maggie put real, old-fashioned, caffeinated tea bags into the mugs. She kept her back to Jane, as if reluctant to begin the conversation without the tea in front of them. Finally, the electric kettle shuddered and burbled, indicating there was water boiling inside. Maggie Reeve poured the tea, offered milk, and fetched it from a small refrigerator. Then she sat down across from Jane at the round white table.

"This is all so new to me," Maggie started. "I don't

know what to do, and I don't have anyone I can talk to."
She smiled. "You're the first person who's asked. So here
goes."

Jane smiled back.

"My dad is Aunt Laura's older brother. He always
looked after her, both before and after she was married to
Edwin. Dad's family was kind of fractured. His father,
my grandfather, was a tyrant. Their mother died when he
and Aunt Laura were small. It left a big hole in their lives.
Their mother was named Margaret, called Meg. Both
Megan and I are named for her. Aunt Laura was never a
strong person mentally or emotionally.

"After Laura's marriage broke up, it was my dad who
took her to the first place she was institutionalized. She
was in a bad way. Every time she got out, he would help
her set up a home, visit her, do errands, and help around
the house. It would last for months, or a couple of years at
the outside, and then the cycle would begin again."

Maggie blew on her tea and took a sip. "Over the
years, she and Dad decided they would remove the things
from her life that tended to send her spiraling. He managed her funds and paid her bills. He picked up her mail
and intercepted any communications from lawyers or
Edwin. Aunt Laura lives . . ." Megan hesitated. "Not far
from here. She has a life. She sells her knitted goods here
in the shop."

"Laura made those?" Jane was impressed. "They are
beautiful."

"They are. And they sell well. They're perfect for the
shop, a luxurious but lower priced item for those who like
to come in and look but can't afford the glass pieces."
Maggie shifted in the plastic chair. "Aunt Laura goes to
book club and yoga. A group of women friends support

her. But she lives in a pretty insular world. She doesn't own a TV or radio or a computer. She doesn't have a cell phone. She has a landline, but only a few people have the number."

"So you don't think she knows her daughter is missing?"

"I'm sure she doesn't. After you called I visited her at her house. She didn't say a word about it, and I'm sure she would have if she knew." Maggie drained her cup in two big gulps. "I don't know whether to tell her. I can't talk to my dad about it. On his bad days he wouldn't understand a word I was saying, and on his good days it would only upset him—about his sister and her daughter—and emphasize how powerless he is to help."

Jane leaned forward and took the woman's thin hand. "You really are alone in this, aren't you?"

She nodded, on the verge of tears. "My parents have been divorced for years. The amount of time and attention Aunt Laura took up was one of many items on my mother's long list of grievances about my father. I can't talk to her. She'd only be incensed that the responsibility she resented my dad having has now fallen on me.

"I'm so torn. Do I keep the news about Megan from my aunt? That seems mean. And what if she finds out in some random way, like when she's here in town, glances at the newsstand, whatever? It would devastate her. It would devastate *me*, and I'm not a mother and recovering alcoholic with a history of breakdowns."

"Can you talk to one of the book group or yoga people, a particular friend, and get their take?" Jane suggested.

Maggie shook her head. "They're not that kind of friend. I think Laura would be mortified if I gave any of them as much information as would be required to have that conversation. I think she likes them because they don't know her history. She can relax and be the person she is today."

Jane shifted in her seat. Maggie was so alone with so much to deal with. "Do you think your aunt wants to know about her daughter? Not this terrible thing, but in general, does she care, or has she put her marriage and child in the past?"

"No, no, no. She cares, she cares. She tried to reconcile with Megan so many times, and then every time she fell apart, and fell off the wagon, she knew she hurt Megan again. So she's given up contacting her. I think she's waiting for some sort of sign that she'll stay clean for good, or something. A sign that may never come. But she loves Megan. My dad used to say that every time Aunt Laura hit bottom it was the thought of Megan that brought her around and got her to fight. She loves Megan. And the pain she has caused Megan is the source of most of her pain."

"Is your aunt in active recovery? Does she have a sponsor?"

"If you're asking if she goes to AA meetings, she does. I think she has a sponsor. What do you think I should do?"

This young woman had asked for her advice, and Jane had to give it. She had walked into this delicate, tragic situation voluntarily. She sat up straight. "I think, and I say this as a mother, you need to tell your aunt what's going on. Keeping it from her will be worse. As you say, she could find out on her own. And if the worst happens"—now it was Jane who faltered, her voice thick—"you will have to tell her, and the whole story will come out. It's better to tell her now."

Maggie's bony shoulders relaxed. "I think so too. I know it's the right thing to do, I just haven't had the courage." She cleared her throat. A delicate *hut-hem*. "My dad was the one who told her about his illness, back while he still could. It was a blow to her. They've always been so close, but she survived it. It didn't send her off the rails, still hasn't even now when he's so much worse."

"She may be stronger than you realize."

Maggie looked directly at her. "Will you come with me?"

Jane tried not to look surprised. "Do you think, from all you've said about your aunt, she would want a stranger present for this conversation?"

"I know her well enough to know she's going to have questions. Lots and lots of questions. I can't answer any of them. Not about the investigation or about Megan and her life. My telling her about Megan's disappearance is going to turn Aunt Laura into an anxious mess. You can at least make sure she has accurate information."

Jane could see her logic. "If you think so, I'll come, of course."

Chapter Thirty-three

Jane waited while Maggie called an employee to come in and cover the shop. At Maggie's direction, Jane moved her car to the small lot that belonged to the store. While Jane did that, Maggie called her aunt to confirm that she was home and tell her she was bringing a visitor. Then Jane and Maggie climbed into Maggie's VW bug. They were out of town and onto a winding country road in less than a minute.

Jane had originally wanted to follow Maggie in her own car, in case Laura Reeve didn't want to see her, but Maggie had argued against it. Now, as Maggie sped down the back roads, careening around turns onto new roads that seemed to leap out of the dense woods without warning, it was everything Jane could do not to brace her hands against the dash.

"You mentioned your dad took care of paying Laura's bills," Jane said, if only to distract herself.

"He did. Now I do."

"Does your aunt have inherited money? Edwin Larsen mentioned that Megan had a trust from your grandfather."

"She does." Maggie responded without taking her eyes off the road, thank goodness. "When my grandfather died, Aunt Laura had already been divorced and through a couple of stints in rehab. He divided the bulk of his money between my dad and a trust for Megan. He set up another, smaller trust for Aunt Laura and made my dad the administrator and trustee."

"Your grandfather didn't trust your aunt with her own money?"

"With good reason, as it turned out. When she was drinking, Aunt Laura could be such a sucker. With the trust, she could tell every person who came to her with a sob story that she didn't have control of her own funds and her mean, mean brother wouldn't give her any money. Which is hilarious, because my dad is probably the softest touch of all. But it worked."

"Megan has a lot of money. The house she bought in Cambridge next to me . . ." Jane paused, not wanting Maggie to think she was wealthy. But then, why would she be embarrassed to have Maggie think that? Money in America was such a tricky thing. "The house Megan bought was quite expensive, and yet from my conversation with her father, I gather there is still money in her trust."

Maggie laughed, a tight-lipped ha ha. "There was originally the same amount in my dad's trust and Megan's, but Edwin has managed Megan's all these years. I assume he understands finance, knows the right people to help invest it. My dad was never interested. Our store has a great reputation. Most of our customers come from

New York, many accompanied by their decorators. Dad supports the sculptors, and we don't lose money, but it's barely more than a hobby. He hasn't invested his money or Laura's aggressively or well. And her hospitalizations have been super expensive, never covered by insurance. Now as we look down the road at the level of care my dad will require, he won't have anything left."

The conversation ended. They were on a long dirt track, barely covered by gravel. It would be a bear in winter ice or spring mud season. There was no dwelling visible until they bumped around a curve and it stood before them, a modest-sized house in a modern farmhouse style, neatly painted an attractive shade of olive green with contrasting dark pink trim. A large lawn at the back of the house rolled down toward a pond.

Jane wasn't sure what she'd been expecting, maybe a modest apartment or tumbledown wreck, a short step up from a halfway house. She knew Laura Reeve had resources—her conversation with Maggie had confirmed it—but she hadn't expected a place that looked so well ordered. Maybe on the inside the chaos of Laura Reeve's life would be visible. But from the outside the house was attractive and well kept, not the home of someone barely managing her life.

Laura came out onto the front porch to meet them, a look of open curiosity on her face. She had passed her tall, slender body to her daughter. When she moved Jane had the sensation of having seen her before. But Laura's chin-length hair had lightened, white streaks among the brown. There were lines around her eyes and in her forehead. She'd had a hard life and it showed.

Maggie parked in the little circle of a drive in front of the porch. Laura approached, hand out. "I'm Laura Reeve."

"Jane Darrowfield."

"Come in, come in." Laura led them through a neat front hall to a charming, rustic kitchen. The inside of the house was as tucked up as the outside. "I made some lemonade. Let's sit on the screened porch." Laura whisked a tray with a pitcher of pale liquid, three glasses filled with ice, and a plate of store-bought cookies off the counter and led them out of the kitchen. Laura might not entertain much, but she was comfortable with company.

The screened porch was large and overlooked the pond. The furniture was comfortable—a deep rattan couch and settee and matching chairs with thick, rust-colored cushions. Knitted items were draped on the chairs and over the back of the couch, all in deep colors, all beautifully made.

Laura cleared a bag filled with breathtaking purple yarn on knitting needles from the settee. Across its back was not another gorgeous knitted throw but a lumpy, amateurish crocheted afghan. Laura spotted Jane staring at it.

"Something I learned in rehab," she said. "Keeps the hands and the mind busy. It helps. This"—she ran her fingers across the afghan—"was my first effort. I keep it to remind myself that big things start with small unsteady steps."

You gave one to your daughter, Jane thought. *She's kept it all these years, despite the estrangement. A symbol of hope.*

Maggie sat next to Laura on the settee. Jane took the chair opposite and accepted the offered glass. There was no point in being impolite. Jane dreaded the conversation to come. It wasn't a cookies and lemonade topic. She wished Maggie had made that clear.

Maggie spoke first. "I've brought Jane here today because she has news about Megan."

Laura shifted on the rattan settee to look more directly at Jane. She appeared surprised, not alarmed.

Jane squared her shoulders and plunged in. It was important to say the worst thing first. Otherwise, after it was told, everything said before it would feel like a lie. "I am so sorry to tell you that Megan is missing."

The impact of the words was instantaneous, as Jane had expected. The color drained from Laura's face; her wide mouth hung open. "What?" she finally managed.

Jane went on. "Megan was last seen at her home in Cambridge on Wednesday night, a week ago tomorrow. By me. I was the last person to see her."

"Megan lives in Cambridge?"

Jane looked at her hands tucked in her lap. Laura Reeve knew even less about her daughter than Jane had supposed. "Yes. She lives next door to me on Birchwood Lane."

"You're her neighbor." Laura seemed momentarily distracted from the headline. Or perhaps she couldn't cope with it.

Jane gently steered her back. "Megan hasn't returned to her home or her office. She hasn't contacted her friends or her father. Cambridge and state police are searching for her. They consider her a missing person."

Laura looked from Jane to Maggie and back, clearly processing. "Do they think Megan"—Laura hesitated, forming the question—"has hurt herself?"

"There's no indication of that," Jane assured her.

"Oh, thank goodness." Tears welled in Laura's eyes and then tracked down her cheeks. "Because I couldn't bear to think . . ." She lost control entirely. Maggie moved beside her aunt on the settee and put her arms around her. Another burden, Jane thought, on this young woman. Comforting an elder. There was a lot on those skinny shoulders.

Jane found an open box of tissues in a powder room off the back hallway and returned with it to the porch. She remembered doing the exact thing at Megan's house a week earlier, after she had told Megan about the gaslighting.

Eventually, sniffling, Laura was ready to go on. "I'm sorry."

"No need. It's upsetting news." It would be devastating to anyone. "I'd like to answer your questions, if I can."

"My Megan . . . is she happy?"

It wasn't the question Jane had expected. It took her a moment to form an answer. "I don't know your daughter well, and she did have some concerns. But yes, in balance, I would say she is happy. She has a good job and a beautiful home. She's very much the mistress of her own life, setting the direction." Or she had been until someone had started messing with her security system and then had abducted her.

"She was always like that, even as a child." Laura smiled through her tears, calmer now. "Maybe she had to be. I wasn't well."

"She's a lawyer, specializing in real estate," Jane added.

Laura nodded, clutching the tissue. "I did know that."

"You have ways of keeping up?"

"Not really, but the last time I saw her was at her law

school graduation. She was studying for the bar exam and had taken a job at the big firm where she'd interned. She told me she loved it. I've pictured her there often. Happy and productive. That has been my wish."

"I think your wish came true."

"She hasn't had . . . any of my problems?"

So they were going to be honest with one another. *Good.* "She isn't an alcoholic, if that's what you're asking. She has recently had some concerns about her mental health, but I think they were unfounded. She worried she was being stalked, and her disappearance would appear to confirm that was the case. She wasn't imagining she was in danger. She was in danger."

"It would have been better if she had imagined it." It was the first time Maggie had contributed to the conversation since her bare-bones introduction.

"Yes," Jane agreed.

"The police think Megan was taken?" Laura asked. "Why?"

"They're pursuing a theory that she might have been abducted," Jane said. "They don't have a motive that I know about. But they haven't ruled out that she might have gone off somewhere without telling anyone, though everyone says it would be very unlike her."

"What has happened, exactly, since Megan has been missing?" Laura asked. "Tell me all the details."

Jane walked them through the last six days, starting with Andy Bromfield's call to the police on Thursday morning. She left out the part of the story that preceded it, the part where Megan came to her asking for help. She elided the discovery of the slipper in the panic room, saying, "At first the police didn't see an adult woman missing a couple of days of work as a problem, but then as time went by, they took the case more seriously."

Laura listened, face solemn.

"Do you have an idea where she would go?" Jane asked.

"No. I'm sorry," Laura said. "I haven't seen Megan in seven years."

"I haven't seen her since I was six years old," Maggie said.

"I'm sorry we met in these circumstances," Jane said. "I'm sorry I brought such bad news."

Laura wiped her eyes. "I'm glad you told me. I feel horrible that she's been missing all this time and I didn't know about it. You will let me know if the police discover"—her voice caught—"anything more." Laura reached for a pad and pen and scrawled her phone number, handing it to Jane.

"I will. But you should also call Detective Tony Alvarez at the Cambridge Police Department. Tell him you're Megan's mother. He'll have questions for you. You can also ask him to let you know as soon as there is any news."

Jane motioned for the pen and pad and wrote Alvarez's name and number followed by her own and then passed it back to Laura, who stared at it as if memorizing it and then put it on the end table next to the settee.

"Megan was an amazing child," Laura said. "So responsible, straight As in school. She'd remind me when it was time to do her homework. But that's how she had to be, the only grown-up in the house. I wasn't a good mother." Laura paused, fighting for control again. "But she was the best daughter a person could ask for."

Jane stood. Maggie jumped up immediately, as if relieved to go. Laura crossed the room and hugged Jane. "Thank you for coming."

She walked them out and stood on the porch while Maggie steered the car down the gravel track. Jane watched in the side mirror until they went around a curve and the house disappeared. Laura had still been on the porch.

Chapter Thirty-four

Jane sat in Old Reliable and stored Maggie's and Laura's contact information in her phone. She glanced at the time and called Alvarez. As the phone rang on speaker, she pulled out of the lot behind the Gallery of Glass and headed toward the turnpike. "Pick up, pick up, pick up," she muttered. She had decided he wasn't going to answer when she heard his voice.

"You've been busy."

"Detective?" What was he talking about?

"I got a call from Megan Larsen's mother fifteen minutes ago."

"Oh." That hadn't taken long, but then Jane hadn't expected it would.

"She told an interesting tale of meeting a neighbor and devoted friend of her daughter who said she should get in touch with me. So if you're calling to give me a heads-up, you're too late."

"Well, I *did* tell her to get in touch with you," Jane said in her own defense. She waited for Alvarez to laugh, but he didn't. "No breaks in the case?"

"As a matter of fact, yes. We've been able to analyze months of logs from the security company. You were right. It appears someone was manipulating Ms. Larsen's home security system. Raising and lowering the thermostat, flashing the lights, opening and closing the garage door in the middle of the night."

Jane's grip tightened on the steering wheel. She had been right. But where did being right get her? How did it help Megan? "Do you know *who* has been harassing her?"

"That will be harder to find. The logs indicated these things were happening, not who was doing them. It's difficult, because whoever was doing it had the correct app with the correct codes. It could have been Ms. Larsen, but that makes no sense, especially in light of her disappearance. I don't understand the ins and outs of it, but the state police have to do a different kind of analysis, not from the security system logs but from the phone records, to find out whose phone it was and where the phone was when it issued the commands."

Alvarez paused, evidently waiting for Jane to speak. When she didn't, he continued. "I've talked to the people you pointed me toward, or most of them, but we have other things we're looking at as well."

"Other people you are looking at," Jane clarified.

"You could say that, but I meant other angles. The digital gaslighting may not be related to the reason Ms. Larsen was taken."

"That seems like a really big coincidence."

"It does," he admitted.

"Who have you talked to? And what did you think?" She was pressing her luck and felt relief when he answered.

"We interviewed the ex-boyfriend."

"Ben Fox. Of course. What did you think?"

"He seems harmless enough. But what I think doesn't come into it. He has an alibi for the night Megan disappeared. A new relationship, apparently. He spent the whole night with her."

"You've talked to the woman and you believe her," Jane confirmed.

"The relationship is so new it seems unlikely she would lie for him. When I told her Fox needed an alibi because his previous girlfriend had disappeared, she didn't blanch. She stated unhesitatingly that he was with her."

"She gave him an alibi. What time, exactly, did he need an alibi for, since the logs on the security system don't show what time Megan left the house?"

"The girlfriend said she and Fox were together the whole night."

This was new information, but Jane had never believed Ben Fox would hurt Megan, either by terrorizing her with her security system or by abducting her. Alvarez had to follow up with the ex, but Jane wasn't surprised by the outcome.

"What about Howard Borg?" she asked.

"We talked to him. He denies knowing anything."

"Do you believe him?"

Alvarez hesitated. "No. Or I'm not sure, at least. I got the same creepy vibe coming off him that you did. But that doesn't make him guilty of abduction. He's hiding something. I don't know what yet. It may not have anything to do with this."

"Just like the digital gaslighting may not have anything to do with Megan's abduction?"

"Touché. I gave the state tech guys all Borg's information."

"What about the former owner, Clark Kinnon?"

"Haven't gotten around to him yet. I'm not sure I see a
connection."

"He has the codes to Megan's system and access to the
phone app."

"If that's true, it only gives him opportunity, and only
for the digital gaslighting. Why would he abduct Megan
Larsen?" It was a reasonable question.

"That leaves someone from Acme," Jane said. "They
have access."

"Who, though, and why?"

"I don't have an answer for the why. But the who
might be either Justin Vreeland, the technician who installed the system and later came out to teach Megan how
to use it, or Agnes Antonucci, the owner."

"Ms. Antonucci and I are old friends at this point. I remember Vreeland from when he let us into the panic
room. I'll see what I can find out about him."

Jane thanked Alvarez for his time. "Have you looked
into Megan's finances? She has a trust fund that paid for
her house."

"We're doing that right now, and that's all I'm willing
to say. I've got to run. There's a team meeting starting
down the hall."

Jane thanked him again, and he was gone.

Chapter Thirty-five

Jane and Harry were both up most of the night. He'd arrived to take up his night watchman duties at about
eight-thirty, though they hadn't previously discussed
whether he'd come over. He'd listened without comment,
but with a deep furrow between his brows, as Jane described her activities of the day.

That night neither of them slept. They were like silent
ships passing as they paced the living room. Each went to
the window so frequently to look out at the dark facade of
Megan's house, Jane thought they'd wear a trough in the
carpet. They knew they wouldn't see anything but were
still compelled to look.

Wembly joined in, too, prowling the downstairs as
they did, careful to stay out of the way of the shuffling,
tired feet. Jane had been trying to guess the cat's age.
Andy had said Wembly was a rescue. He was a mature
cat, that was certain, and Jane suspected that whenever he

was "hiding" during the day he was asleep somewhere comfy. But not that night. He was a watchman, too, just like Harry. Just like Jane.

"If only one of us had been up the night Megan was taken," Jane said. "If only we'd looked out the window." She shook her head. "I have never felt so useless."

"You've been useful. More than. You found Megan's mother."

Jane had to agree with that. "But I don't know what to do now."

Harry put an arm around her. The light cotton of his seersucker bathrobe felt cool on her arm. "Maybe you do nothing more about this case. The police are all over it, Cambridge city, state, and probably the FBI. The media is still covering Megan's disappearance every day."

Jane had to acknowledge he was right, though it didn't feel good.

"Don't you have that other case you can work on?"

"I do." The case of Roo the cat, whose affections were being alienated by Gordon and Pam Marshall. Or at least that's what Ralph Pilchner and his wife thought, though Jane wasn't so sure after speaking with the Marshalls.

"Maybe focus on that."

At six a.m. they both gave up pretending there would be any sleep that night. "I'll go home and get showered and changed," Harry said. "Since there's no room for me to leave any clothes here." His voice was even, neither nagging nor scolding, but it made Jane feel terrible anyway. Why couldn't she do this simple thing for someone she cared about so deeply?

After Harry left, Jane pawed through her closet and opened her drawers. Why was she so certain she needed all this stuff? Even if she had the occasion, would she really want to wear any of it? It was hanging there, slowly going out of style. But she was unable to make a single decision. She closed the closet and the drawers and walked away.

She drank her coffee and ate her solitary breakfast. Wembly had disappeared again, probably getting some much needed shut-eye. Jane stuck her head out her front door. The air was heavy and the sky gray. It had been so long since it had rained, Jane doubted it finally would, but she grabbed her umbrella as she headed out her door.

Ceil Pilchner answered the front door, yelling, "Ralph!" as she held fast to the collar of a barking German shepherd. "This is Bonnie," she explained. "Don't let her scare you. She's a big old baby." Mrs. Pilchner backed up so Jane could enter as Ralph came down the staircase behind her.

The front hall opened into a large light living room that was strewn from one end to the other with colorful toys, superheroes, Barbies, Legos, and puzzles. The Pilchners' grandchildren had not so much moved in as taken over. Mrs. Pilchner kicked toys steadily out of Jane's path as they entered the room. Bonnie sniffed and then licked Jane's hand, which evidently was the signal for Mrs. Pilchner to let her collar go. The dog sniffed Jane one last time and then decided she was okay and retreated to a dog bed in a corner.

"Welcome! Welcome!" Ralph boomed. "Ceil, Jane's the one who's working on our Roo problem. Have you been able to talk to those Marshalls yet?" As he spoke, he gestured for Jane to sit in an overstuffed chair.

Jane moved aside a doll in a costume from a movie or TV show she was vaguely aware of but had never seen. "I did," she confirmed.

"And?" Ralph also cleared a place and sat on the couch, as did Ceil.

"The Marshalls are entirely sympathetic with your feelings."

"Good." Ralph seemed impressed. "Then they'll stop feeding Roo and send her home?"

Jane leaned forward. "It may not be quite so simple. The Marshalls claim they didn't entice Roo away from your home, she more or less fled."

"Fled? That's ridiculous. Are they saying we mistreated her? Because we never . . ." Ceil was incensed.

"Nothing like that." Jane reassured her. "It's . . ." Jane paused and looked around the chaos of the room. "I understand your grandchildren have come to stay, along with your son."

"They have not come to stay." Ceil was vehement. "They are *visiting*."

Ralph glanced sideways at his wife with an expression Jane couldn't read—perhaps a mix of exasperation and pity. "We don't know how long they're here for," he told Jane. "Our son is experiencing marital difficulties."

"That has nothing to do with the cat! Those Marshalls don't get to have our cat because there's a few extra people here for a short period of time." Ralph might be uncertain about the change in their household—how long it would last, and what the impact was—but Ceil was not.

"And pets," Jane added. "Bonnie here, and I understand there's another cat. How long have they all been here?"

"Since the beginning of the summer," Ralph answered.

"About the time that Roo started spending so much time next door?" Jane suggested.

"No!" Ceil jumped up from the sofa. "Just because my

grandchildren are here, the Marshalls don't get to have *my* cat." She pointed at Jane from the other side of the room. "You go back over there and you tell them I want my cat back. *Right now.*" And then she stomped out of the room. Moments later, the sound of aggressive dishwashing echoed from the kitchen. There didn't seem to be anything else to say. Jane got to her feet.

"Sorry about that," Ralph said as he walked her to the front door.

"Don't apologize. Your wife is obviously under a great deal of stress."

"He's our son," Ralph explained. "They're our grandchildren. They needed someplace to go. How could we say no?"

"I understand." Jane looked down the street. "Have you ever seen a big black SUV parked at the end of your road?"

"Lots of times."

"Does it belong to anyone, do you know?"

"I don't think so, because I've asked."

The car had aroused the curiosity of more than one neighbor. "Who lives down there?" Jane asked.

Ralph pointed. "That house is empty most of the time. Foreign investor. Same with the one next to it on the right. On the left are Joe and Phil. Nice couple. Both work from home. Then next house nearest us are the Presleys, Nancy and Connor."

"I've met them," Jane said, though she couldn't quite remember where. Connor was some kind of a big deal in the city. Nancy was home, the attractive, capable wife.

"I figure it's a commuter who catches the trolley on Mount Auburn," Ralph said. There hadn't been a streetcar running down the middle of Mount Auburn Street for more than sixty years, but like most natives, Ralph called the electrified buses that had replaced the streetcars trolleys.

"So the SUV is here only during the day?" Jane looked up Old Deer Path toward Megan's house. Megan would have been at her office, not at home during the day, so what would be the point of watching her house?

"Sometimes it's parked overnight," Ralph said. "But rarely. Like maybe the owner is on a business trip or something."

"And you've never seen the owner."

"I didn't say that."

Jane's heart beat a little faster. "Man or a woman?"

"Man. Definitely. Business type. Middle-aged. Middle height. Sturdy build. Not anyone you'd notice. I've called out to him a few times. 'Hey, you can't park there.' That sort of thing. He ignores me."

"And you don't see where he goes?"

"Toward Birchwood Lane, then around the corner. That's all I know."

"You never photographed the license or called it in to the police?"

"Nah. He's not really bothering anyone when it comes down to it. Why should we all be calling the police on one another? That's no way to live."

"Have you seen the SUV since Megan Larsen disappeared?"

Ralph rubbed his chin. "Come to think of it, no. Do you think it has something to do with her?"

"I don't know. Maybe it's suspicious that a car was parked day after day with a perfect view of Megan's house. Will you call me if it shows up again?"

"Sure. Sure. My wife's already nervous about a neighbor disappearing in the middle of the night. It has us all on edge, especially with the grandkids in the house."

The air was still heavy. Jane could smell the rain. But it hadn't come yet.

"It's just she's so upset," Ralph said. "All the noise and confusion, the barking and the mess. And not knowing how long it's going to last. It's been two adults for so long. A quiet, tidy house. It's an adjustment."

"I understand."

Jane was off his stoop and walking down the street before she realized she didn't know if Ralph had been talking about his wife or his cat.

Chapter Thirty-six

Jane didn't go directly to the Marshalls' house from the Pilchners. It was too provocative, too reactive. She hadn't figured out what she planned to say. Instead she stood on Old Deer Path and surveyed the houses at the end of the street. Ralph had said that two of them were essentially empty, owned by foreign investors. Jane went up the front walk of the one closer to the Pilchners and rang the bell, which echoed loudly. No footsteps came. On the window nearest the front door, a sticker read ACME SECURITY. Like the one at Megan's house. Jane hurried to the other empty house Pilchner had pointed out. It had an Acme sticker too.

There had to be at least a dozen of these vacant houses in the neighborhood. Maybe more. Wouldn't one of them be the perfect place to hide someone, especially someone abducted from nearby in the middle of the night? Did all the new fancy renos have panic rooms like Megan's did?

Walking along the curving roads of her neighborhood, Jane inspected every one of the empty houses, peering in the ground floor windows. Each was fully and expensively furnished, a place anyone would be happy to come home to. Except no one ever did. Every single one had an Acme Security sticker on its front window.

Jane returned to her house, left the umbrella, grabbed her pocketbook, and drove to Acme. She had a feeling the formidable Agnes would be more inclined to answer her questions in person rather than over the phone.

The Acme building was a low-slung warehouse behind the Whole Foods in Fresh Pond. The road it faced, called New Street, was the sneaky back way into the stores, banks, and restaurants on both sides of the perpetually jammed Fresh Pond Parkway. Jane knew the little cut-through well but had never noticed the Acme building. Plate glass windows and a glass door in a corner of the front indicated the office. There wasn't much parking, and the building facade was more formidable than welcoming. This wasn't a place that clients visited often. It was the place the technicians loaded up their trucks, where the inventory was kept, and where phone calls were answered.

Agnes was on the phone at the front desk in the cluttered office. She was neither young nor old but somewhere in middle age, blowing both of Jane's theories about where her name might have come from. She was petite—more than petite, she was tiny—and yet somehow scary and very much in charge.

Agnes motioned for Jane to wait on a dusty couch on

the other side of the small room. Jane sat, thinking she would have to change her khaki skirt as soon as she got home. Eavesdropping on Agnes's call wasn't illuminating or even interesting. She was ordering stock in a language that was barely English. At one point she was apparently asked to clarify and shouted into the phone, "No! Not eighty 20DX40s, forty 20DX80s!" She wiggled her eyebrows at Jane, clearly exasperated. She listened some more, silently nodding, and then said, "I have to go. I have someone in my office."

When she hung up, Jane approached her desk and sat in the utilitarian chrome and plastic chair in front of it. "I'm Jane Darrowfield," she said. "We spoke on the phone about my neighbor's security system."

"Your neighbor who disappeared." Agnes nodded, her mouth a grim line. "Believe me, I remember. The police made us turn over our logs, and they've followed up many times with questions. So time-consuming. Whatever happened to your neighbor, I have assured the police, several times, had nothing to do with us."

"I noticed you do a lot of business in my neighborhood."

"We do a lot of business all over the Boston metro area. What's it to you?"

Agnes was overly aggressive. Jane expected to be invited out of the office at any moment. "A lot of the houses with your systems in my area are empty, owned by foreign investors who are seldom there."

"That's why they need good security systems."

"Yes, I understand. I wondered, do you ever check the properties physically, send out guards to patrol them, or do you only install and monitor alarms?"

"We don't offer patrol services. We will go to a house

if there's a problem and the homeowner has given us in-structions to do so. For example, if the system has indi-cated there's no heat or a leak somewhere. And of course if the security alarm goes off or the homeowner calls us."

"Who would go out? A technician?"

"Exactly. If it's something routine. If it appears to be a break-in or a fire or other emergency, we contact first re-sponders and then our technician follows up at the scene."

"That would be a technician like Justin Vreeland, who came out to open Megan Larsen's panic room?"

"It would be a technician exactly like Justin Vreeland. In your neighborhood it would often be Justin."

"I'd like to speak to Mr. Vreeland. Is he available?"

"He is not. Why do you want to talk to him?"

"There are some things about the security system I don't understand, and since I'm looking after Megan's house, I need to know them."

"Really? You're looking after Ms. Larsen's house? I would think that would be the police."

Jane backtracked. "I'm taking care of Megan's cat at the request of the police, and that requires me to visit the house frequently to retrieve his food and supplies."

"Mmm-hmm." Agnes plainly wasn't buying it. "I'm afraid you can't talk to Justin regardless of the reason. He's off today."

She sounded annoyed. Jane wasn't sure if she was an-noyed at her or at Justin, but she took a chance. "He's on a regular vacation day?"

Agnes's ire got the better of her. "It's getting to be a regular vacation day, but no, that's not what I meant. Every so often Justin doesn't show up for work. He claims he's sick, but I know he's not. He's always back the next day good as new with some story about food poisoning or a twenty-four-hour bug. He doesn't even have the good grace to call me himself. He has his wife call, and you know who has to reschedule all his appointments and make excuses to the homeowners and businesses? Me."

"That must not be fun," Jane sympathized.

"It is not! You try explaining to somebody who re-arranged all *their* meetings to take a day off from work to wait for the technician that now you're rescheduling *your* appointments. It doesn't go well. I can tell you that."

"I imagine it doesn't."

"I would fire him," Agnes continued, "but except for a few 'sick days' he's my best employee. He cares deeply about the safety and security of our homeowners. I call him 'Justin the Guardian.' I joke it's his superhero name."

Jane stood to go. "If you hear from him, would you tell him to give me a call? I have a couple of questions."

Agnes said, "Will do." But Jane doubted she would. As Agnes had said, why was Jane asking questions?

Chapter Thirty-seven

Jane pulled her car out of the lot that was so plainly visible through Acme Security's front windows and drove down New Street into the Whole Foods parking lot. Half the parked cars had drivers inside them fiddling with their phones. Jane fit right in.

Taking her cue from Agnes, Jane was convinced Justin Vreeland wasn't ill. But what was he doing? She had started off wanting to talk to him about the empty houses in her neighborhood. Now curiosity drove her on.

It didn't take Jane long to find his home address on the Internet. He lived in Tewksbury, almost an hour away. Even though Jane was feeling the effects of her sleepless night, she was determined to go. Jane had time, something Megan was possibly running out of.

Justin lived in a hilly area of long winding two-lane roads. Jane turned off the road and steered along the steep dirt track that served as a driveway to the Vreeland house.

The house was a weird hybrid—part A-frame, part log cabin with a newish wood frame addition. It looked thrown together and homemade. Bikes and other toy vehicles were lined up neatly at the top of the drive. The house was so far off the road there was little chance anything left outside would be stolen.

Jane stopped Old Reliable a ways from the house. The clouds had burned off without producing the promised rain, and the sky was bright blue, the sun blazing and relentless. Jane stood, hands on her hips, suddenly reluctant to go on. Why was she doing this? But then the twitch of a blind on a big picture window told her she'd been spotted. It would be infinitely weirder to turn around and drive back down the long driveway than to climb the rickety wooden stairs, knock on the door, and state her business. Justin was a security tech, so it seemed likely the occupants of the house had seen her coming from the time she turned off the main road, though she hadn't spotted the cameras that must be in the trees that lined the driveway.

Jane climbed the stairs, treading carefully on the weather-beaten wood.

"May I help you?" The woman who answered the door was in her middle thirties, but already showing signs of age, a slight stoop in her posture and a sag to her cheeks and chin. Her hair was a dull, sandy color, tied in a low ponytail.

"Mrs. Vreeland?" Jane ventured.

"Yes."

"I'm Jane Darrowfield. I met your husband at one of the houses that Acme services."

The woman squinted into the sun. "If this is about home

security, you really need to go to the Acme office. Justin doesn't do any business from here."

There was a whoop behind her, followed by a high-pitched squeal. Both women waited silently to see if the squeal turned to laughter or tears. Instead there was a crash and a scream of surprise.

Jane took a chance. "May I come in?" She stated her name again, offering her hand this time.

The woman glanced back into the house, clearly torn. She would have preferred to stay on the doorstep, but that risked mayhem inside. "I'm Crystal," she said, taking the offered hand. "Come on in."

Crystal. The name was appropriate to her age but not her face. Did parents know when they gave their children these shiny names that they would grow into careworn adults?

There were three children that Jane could see, a girl and a boy dressed like they weren't long home from elementary school and a little one wearing only a T-shirt and pull-up training pants. The house was hot and stuffy. Crystal shooed the children out of the kitchen to watch TV, an offer that was met with eyes opened in surprise. Clearly not the usual afternoon directive.

The house was neat, much neater than Jane expected given three active children in residence. Her mind flashed to the Pilchner house, where toys were everywhere. Crystal cleared the leavings from an after-school snack—apples spread with peanut butter—from the kitchen table and gestured Jane toward a chair. "Please sit. How can I help you?"

"I'm looking for Justin. I called Acme, and they told me he was home sick."

"They shouldn't have sent you here."

Of course they hadn't. "I'm taking care of a neighbor's house and it has a system Justin installed and maintained, so that's why the Acme office couldn't answer my questions."

"Hmmpf." Crystal had seated herself at the head of the table, catty-corner from Jane. "They rely on him way too much. It isn't fair."

"Is he here? I understood he was sick."

Crystal colored slightly. "No. He's out. He's off." She gestured, flinging out an arm, as if he might be orbiting the earth.

"So not sick, then?"

"Maybe not physically." Crystal made a face. "But sick of them and that place." She settled in her chair. The sounds of cartoon characters running amuck came from the living room. "It's so unfair. Not only does he work for them eight hours every day, he also does installations for businesses on the weekends. And they feel they can get him out of bed any hour of the night if an alarm goes off somewhere or there's a problem with someone's system. Usually they call and he races to the house and the cops are already there with the EMTs and it turns out a raccoon tripped an alarm or some other thing."

"I can see that it's a demanding job."

"And that's not even the worst of it. When Justin's home, supposedly on his time off, he has to keep checking and monitoring the system. He spends his day in that truck and then his evenings in his little study in the basement staring at his computer. It's not right."

"My goodness, doesn't anyone else work at Acme?"

Crystal grimaced. "I know. Right? That's what I say.

Justin says all the techs work that way, but I don't believe him. Agnes, the owner, calls him 'Justin the Guardian.'"

"So where is he?" Jane asked.

"Fishing. Every once in a while he takes a mental health day and goes off."

"And you cover for him?"

"He deserves it. No one can work twenty-four-seven for months on end like Agnes expects."

"Does Justin have a boat, perhaps on a lake nearby?"

"No, no. He's fly-fishing on a stream in the woods. It totally relaxes him."

Really? It was fall, in the midst of a long drought. The water would be trickling, not rushing, and the stocks fished out. Jane doubted very much Justin could be fly-fishing. But if his main objective was to get away from the demands of home and work, then maybe it didn't matter. Maybe he stood in the woods with a pole and that did the trick. "Does he have a place he goes?"

"Maine," Crystal said. "It makes me nervous that he goes out of cell range, in case something happens with the kids, but it's the only way he can get any peace."

Jane stood. "When do you expect him? My questions about my neighbor's security system are urgent." She opened her pocketbook and handed Crystal a card. Not the fancy cards Harry had made for her that she gave to clients, the ones that said PROFESSIONAL BUSYBODY. This one was a plain white card with her name, cell phone number, and e-mail address. These cards were for sources, such as Crystal.

Crystal took the card, but she hesitated before she did. "Why can't your neighbor give you the information you need?"

That was the question. "She's disappeared," Jane answered.

"You mean that woman! It's been on the news all the time. Justin told me he worked on the system at her house. He was over there recently because some old lady—" Crystal stopped, embarrassed.

"That was me," Jane admitted. "That's how we met. That's why I thought he might be willing to answer my questions."

"Shouldn't the police be asking the questions?"

"This isn't about the search for Megan. This is more about the house. That's why it's me doing the asking. Have the police talked to Justin?"

Crystal's already pale skin turned paler. "No. Why would they?"

"No reason." Jane tried to sound casual. "I thought they might have questions about the security system."

"They haven't talked to Justin. He would have told me. Maybe they got all the information they needed from Agnes."

"Maybe they did."

The youngest child came into the kitchen, clutching a worn blanket that might at some time have been white. "Kyle won't play with me."

"You can help me make dinner," Crystal said. "You can stir things in the big bowl."

The little boy smiled, accepting the alternative.

"I'll see myself out," Jane said.

"Bye! Sorry I couldn't be more help," Crystal called after her.

Chapter Thirty-eight

By the time she reached the highway, Jane's energy was flagging. She called Alvarez. "Did you know there are more than a dozen empty houses in my neighborhood?" she asked him.

"I imagine there would be. Your area has always been home to college professors, people who can go away for the summer months. And retirees who may be away in the winter."

"I mean right now, in September, a dozen empty houses. It used to be a neighborhood of academics, but now it's a neighborhood of investors, people who need to move money out of their countries and think Cambridge real estate is a good place to park it. These houses are hardly ever lived in."

"What are you saying?"

"I think you should search every last one for Megan.

Wouldn't that be a great place to stash someone you took from her home in the middle of the night?"

Alvarez was quiet. Finally, he said, "You want us to get permission from a dozen foreign nationals to search their unoccupied homes?"

"I think it's important. All of these homes have Acme security systems, and the technician who came to Megan's house to let you into the panic room, the person who has serviced most of those houses, has disappeared. You need to find him."

"Disappeared? Has he been reported missing?" The detective sounded alarmed.

"His wife says he's fishing."

"So, no." Alvarez's voice returned to normal. "Where is he fishing?"

"In Maine."

"We need to find someone who is fishing somewhere in the entire state of Maine?"

"He can't be that far north in Maine if he's expected back tonight." It sounded lame to Jane even as she said it, but she rushed on. "And there's a black SUV that's been hanging around the neighborhood. You need to track that down too."

"You want me to find a man somewhere in Maine," he repeated, "and a black SUV somewhere in greater Boston. Is that what you're saying?" It sounded ridiculous when he said it.

"In the southern part of Maine," Jane insisted. "Megan is such a nice person," she blurted. "And young. She has her whole life ahead of her. And her mother is fragile. She's doing okay, but if we don't find Megan, I can't even think about what it will do to her mother." Jane's voice quavered, shocking her. Where had that come from? She inhaled deeply, fighting for control.

"Jane, what are you doing right now?" Alvarez sounded stern and worried.

"I'm driving. I'm on 93 headed to my house."

"Pull over." It was an order.

"What?"

"Pull over to the shoulder and stop your car. You shouldn't be driving."

"What?" What was he talking about? Jane put on her blinker and edged toward the right lane.

"Are you doing what I said?"

She pulled onto the shoulder and stopped the car. The dam broke. As soon as the car engine was off, Jane began to sob. "Tony, what did I do? I told her to turn off the cameras!"

"Stay there. Cry it all out before you drive again. Do you need me to send someone to pick you up?"

"No! I'm fine." What a mortifying idea. "I didn't sleep at all last night and I'm tired and worried . . ."

"You're not fine. None of this is fine. Pull yourself together, go home, and get some sleep."

The fight had gone out of her. "I will."

"Promise?"

"I promise, Tony. Thank you. Will you see about searching those empty houses?"

Alvarez had the grace to laugh. "You never give up, do you? Let me run it by the team."

Chapter Thirty-nine

Jane pulled herself together and edged back onto Route 93. It was the thick of rush hour. She was traveling toward the city, not away from it, but in the last few years rush hour had become a bidirectional crawl that lasted most of the day. When she finally let herself in her back door, the sleepless night, emotional outburst, and sheer frustration at her helplessness had taken a heavy toll. It was still light out, but barely. She kicked off her canvas shoes, dished out food and clean water for Wembly, and fell gratefully onto her bed. She slept deeply and dreamlessly.

The sun streamed in the windows when she was awakened by the sound of slamming car doors. She looked out into the street. Two patrol cars, along with Alvarez's unmarked Cambridge city car and a white van with the Acme Security logo on it, were parked on the street. As Jane watched, Detective Alvarez and Justin Vreeland, trailed by two uniformed officers, went up the driveway of the vacant house nearest her home. Vreeland hit the keypad outside the garage door. The door went up, and they proceeded inside.

So they had listened to her. Alvarez did think it was a good lead. She hurried to clean up and dress. She was still in yesterday's clothes.

She took her coffee out onto her front steps to watch the progress of the search. The police were moving through the vacant houses with impressive efficiency. It was only when she sat down on her stoop that she thought to look at her phone.

There were eight texts from Gordon Marshall starting at 8:36 the previous night.

The black suv is here!

Then: **Are you coming?**

Then immediately: **No don't come. Too dangerous. Abductor on the loose.**

Then: **What was I thinking?** 🤔

Then: **I'll try to get a photo.**

Followed by a fuzzy dark image of a hulking black SUV parked across the street from the Marshalls' house.

Then: **Did you get it?**

And finally: **I guess you're out somewhere. At least I hope so. Ha ha!**

And then, at 11:13 p.m., there was a text from Harry:

Came over. You asleep. Better to let you be. Call me.

Jane was flooded with warmth that Harry had come to look in on her, followed by shivers that he'd been walking around her house while she was sleeping and she'd had no idea. Is that what happened to Megan? No, she woke up before she was taken. The slippers proved it.

Looking down Old Deer Path, Jane spotted Gordon

and Pam Marshall on their front steps. Half the neighborhood, the half that wasn't at work or in some country on
the other side of the world, was outside watching the police move from house to house. Gordon waved, and Jane
walked toward them.

"Did you get my texts? Were they helpful?" he called.

Gordon was so eager; Jane didn't want to tell him the
photo was useless. "I'll show it to the detective today.
You didn't happen to take a picture of the license plate,
did you?"

Gordon shook his head. "No way I'm skulking around
outdoors after dark when there's someone out there snatch-
ing people. I sent what I could get from right here." He
pointed down at the stoop where he stood. He seemed a
little peeved that she would even ask.

"Got it. Got it. Of course."

Next door, Ralph Pilchner stepped onto his stoop to
watch the proceedings. Ceil came out behind him, but as
soon as she spotted the Marshalls, she whirled around
and went back inside.

I've got to do something about that, Jane thought. *So
sad; they used to be friends.*

Alvarez, the two uniformed policemen, and Justin
Vreeland in his Acme coveralls came out of one of the
empty houses at the end of Old Deer Path and walked toward the next one. Alvarez nodded his head to Jane in ac-
knowledgment.

She walked home to find Helen and Phyllis sitting on
her front steps.

"I can't stand this." Phyllis hugged herself.

"It is upsetting." For Helen, this admission constituted
an emotional outburst.

Jane nodded and joined them.

An hour later, Alvarez came by accompanied by a youngish cop in uniform. The detective shook his head. "Nothing, Jane. Sorry."

That was disappointing. "*I'm* sorry I wasted your time."

"It was a good idea, just not the right one." Behind them, Vreeland got in his Acme van and drove away. "It was easier to get permission to enter the houses than I expected. Agnes at Acme was really helpful in contacting the owners."

"Those houses are creepy, man." The younger cop shook his head. "Like a movie set waiting for the actors. Nobody's home."

"You're right," Phyllis said. "They're nobodies' homes."

"Thank you for trying," Jane said. "We're all on edge here."

"The whole city's on edge. The publicity is good. It's keeping Megan Larsen top of mind, but it's freaking everyone out."

"You don't think we have anything to worry about?" Helen asked.

"I don't." Alvarez appeared to have no doubt. "We believe whatever happened to Megan came from her life. It wasn't random."

"That's a relief." Phyllis spoke for all of them.

Jane came off the steps and held out her phone. "My neighbor took this photo of an SUV that's been parked near his house a lot. The one I told you about." Jane pointed down Old Deer Path. "It parks right there. For hours apparently. As you can see, it's a straight view from the car to Megan's house."

Alvarez took the phone and squinted at the image. "Did someone sit in the car for long periods of time watching her house?"

"I don't think so. At least my neighbors didn't mention it. One of them said the owner is a middle-aged man. He thinks he might be a commuter. I'm sorry the photo's so terrible. It was dark."

"Send me these neighbors' names and contact information. I'll have someone talk to them. But don't expect anything to happen right away. We're stretched pretty thin."

"Thanks." After the morning's wasted efforts, the police weren't going to be jumping on her leads anytime soon.

The uniformed officer leaned in to examine the blurry photo on the phone. "Cadillac Escalade." He looked at their astonished faces and grinned. "Three years in Traffic."

"We've got to get going. Ladies." Alvarez gave a slight bow.

They watched the men get into their cars and drive away.

"What's wrong?" Helen asked Jane.

She hadn't realized what her feelings were, much less that they were on her face. "I'm disappointed. I thought searching the empty houses was a good idea. I'm worried. I'm frustrated." She cast around for words.

"That's it," Phyllis said. "We're going to lunch. I need to get out of this neighborhood for a while. I'll call Irma." She looked at Jane. "You drive."

Chapter Forty

Jane drove over Walden Street toward Irma's house. From the back seat Phyllis regaled Helen with the story of how she had discovered Ralph Pilchner and delivered the case of his affectionately alienated cat to Jane. Jane listened with half her attention, keeping her eyes on the other Massachusetts drivers ahead of her as they turned without signaling, rushed in multicar formations through lights no longer yellow, and honked at everything and everyone. The usual.

She didn't make it through the light at Walden and Garden Street on the first cycle. Why were all these people driving around in the middle of the day? Why weren't they at work? Jane pulled to the front of the line of cars and stopped. She looked idly over at the parking lot of Clark Kinnon Homes. She'd passed it so many times, but now that she'd been inside she stared at the building, deeply curious.

A black SUV with Massachusetts plates was parked in front. From across the street, Jane couldn't read its logo or the name of the make, which was written in stylized metal. Was it a Cadillac? A shiver shot through her. *Calm down*, she told herself. Black SUVs were a dime a dozen. But the Escalade was so enormous, so crazy and impractical for Cambridge with its narrow streets and tiny parking spaces. How many could there be? Did she remember it parked in the torn-up driveway next door while the house was being renovated? She thought perhaps she did.

The light changed at last. Jane stepped on the gas, only to get caught on the other side in a line of cars waiting at the next light. Progress was agonizingly slow. Finally they turned onto Irma's block of two-family houses facing a park. Irma was on her front porch. When she saw them she waved and came down the steps.

"Where are we headed?" she asked when she got in the car.

"Cambridge Common. Great burgers, great salads, and there's parking," Phyllis pronounced.

After much maneuvering around the dividing island of Mass Ave, they pulled up at the restaurant. As the others opened their doors to get out, Jane said, "I forgot something at home. You go ahead and order. I'll be right back."

"It will take you half an hour to get home and get back," Phyllis responded. "Whatever it is, forget about it."

"Get started with the gossip portion," Jane said. "I'll be here before you know it."

She didn't rush to Clark Kinnon Homes, because rushing wasn't possible, but she was more aggressive than she'd been on the way over, skittling through a light formerly yellow, not caring if she blocked an intersection. Now she was the jerk.

When she approached Kinnon's building going the other way, she didn't get stopped by the light. Cars were right on her tail, so she had to keep going. The big SUV was still there, but she was driving too fast to read the logo or the word in script on the back. She had to go around the block, which in Cambridge meant going around five blocks. From somewhere deep in her pocketbook her cell phone rang. She didn't take the time to fish it out. At last, she approached the building and pulled into the parking lot. She drove slowly up behind the car. *Escalade*, the script read. *Bingo*. Jane parked and went inside.

Gloria Zinn was at her place behind the reception desk. "Yes?"

"I'm here to see Clark," Jane announced.

"Do you have an appointment? Whom shall I say is inquiring?"

"You know who I am, and you know I don't have an appointment."

"I'll have to check to see if he's in."

"He's in," Jane said. "His car's out front." It was an educated guess. She didn't know for sure it was Clark's car. What if it was Ms. Zinn's and she was the one stalking Megan? What kind of convoluted story would that be?

Ms. Zinn disappeared down the hall without an argument, so one of the cars in the parking lot for sure was Clark's. She came back looking mildly surprised. "He says for you to go on in."

Jane walked down the dark hallway. The lights were off like the last time she'd been there. *What's up with this,* she wondered once again.

He sat behind his desk, staring at his computer monitor. "You'll excuse me if I don't get up."

"Yes, certainly, I'll excuse you. For that."

He turned his attention to her. "What can I do for you, Mrs. Darrowfield?"

Jane remained standing. "I'm here to talk about Megan Larsen."

He half laughed, half snorted. "She's a nice lady I sold a house to once. I explained that to you."

"And that's all you know about her? I don't believe you."

He shrugged his square shoulders. "That's all I know for a fact. A number of my fellow developers use Booker-man, Digby, and Eade as their law firm. There's been a lot of talk, speculation, and rumors."

"What sort of rumors?" Jane hadn't meant her tone to be so sharp.

"You know. She ran away, she killed herself, she was kidnapped, she was abducted by aliens. Nothing based in any sort of fact."

"Have the police spoken to you?" Jane asked

"I had a call from a detective yesterday in the late af-ternoon. He asked me the same thing you did. Did I have any of the codes for Ms. Larsen's house? I told him the same thing I told you. I had the codes to enter the house, which I did frequently during interior construction. I have no idea if she changed them. I haven't attempted to use them any time since."

Jane shifted from foot to foot. This was where the rub-ber met the road. "So you did tell me. But since we last talked, I've learned that after Megan's house was sold, your car has been seen parked on Old Deer Path on a reg-ular basis."

Kinnon's face flushed. His mouth opened as if he was about to yell. But then he thought better of it. Instead he jumped to his feet and closed his office door, looking out into the hallway before he did so. Turning back to Jane he said, "Look, I don't know who you really are or what you think you're up to, but if my car was parked on Old Deer Path, as you allege, I can assure you the reason had nothing to do with Megan Larsen."

"You can assure me all you like, and then you can assure the police when they come around and ask the same questions."

That slowed him down. "Why would they?"

Jane sat perfectly still. "Because I sent them a photo of your car in situ."

"You what?! Why in the name of heaven would you do that?"

"Because Megan Larsen is missing. Prior to going missing, she was being harassed via her home security system. You have the codes to that system, and your car has been frequently parked perfectly positioned to watch her house. The question, I think, is why *wouldn't* the police talk to you?"

The effect of this speech on Kinnon was immediate and visible. His face, which had paled from its peak color, flushed again. His mouth opened and closed several times. "Who are you, and why is it your goal to harass me? Did my wife send you?"

An unexpected response. "Your wife?" When Kinnon didn't answer, Jane said, "Mr. Kinnon, I assure you I've never met your wife. If you were doing something you'd rather she didn't know about, you're better off telling the police about it now. It's better to be suspected of infidelity than abduction or murder. Were you having an affair with Megan Larsen?"

"Good grief, no! I told you, I barely knew the woman. She bought a house from my company. We sell a lot of houses."

Jane's cell phone rattled in her bag. She ignored it. "Then what were you doing parked on Old Deer Path?"

Kinnon grimaced and stared at the floor. "It is what you think." His voice was low. "I am involved with a woman in your neighborhood, but I assure you, she is not Megan Larsen."

"Is this woman, this other woman, willing to tell the police why you're parked on a street with a direct line of sight to Megan's house?"

His eyebrows flew up his forehead. "Do you think that will be necessary?"

"I do."

The eyebrows came down. "You see, my friend is married too, and this could be most . . . inconvenient."

"I'm sure the police will be discreet. Unless you took Megan Larsen, in which case they won't be."

"I've told you, nothing like that. As a matter of fact, I did meet my friend when I was renovating the house on Birchwood Lane. I was there frequently to check on progress, and she was often outside tending her garden."

Jane's mind traveled, picturing the immediate neighbors on her street. She eliminated one house because of its scruffy front garden. No one would have been outside tending it. Then she eliminated a much older couple, both at home, and two working couples, never home, who used professional landscapers. Next was one of the empty houses, occupied only by the children of Saudi royalty during the school holidays. Through this process of elimination it was easy to figure out who Kinnon's paramour must be.

"We got to talking," Kinnon continued. "There was a spark, an undeniable spark. One thing led to another."

Was he telling the truth? He was clearly embarrassed. Not you-caught-me-in-a-crime embarrassed, but you-caught-me-committing-adultery embarrassed. When she'd worked, Jane had always been astonished by coworkers who had affairs. *Where do they find the time?* But Kinnon was the master of his own schedule, out and about frequently checking on projects. And the neighbor Jane imagined was having the affair with him was home alone all the time while her husband kept them in that expensive house.

Jane stood. "Mr. Kinnon, what you do in your personal life is none of my business, as you say. But Megan Larsen is my business, and if you can help clear up anything related to her disappearance, I suggest you speak to the police again before they contact you. And before you call them, spend some time thinking about anything you might have observed during all that time you spent in the neighborhood." She paused. "I'll see myself out."

Chapter Forty-one

When Jane was back in her car, she pulled out her cell phone. Four calls from Phyllis and ten texts expressing increasing alarm. The final one said, **Where are you? There is a person taking women in our neighborhood. If you don't text back in ten seconds I'm calling Harry.**

It had been sent twenty minutes earlier.

Oh no. Jane called right back. "Don't call Harry," she begged.

"Too late," Phyllis replied. "He's here in the restaurant."

"He's there?"

"We thought you were dead, so all of us who love you should be together. Hold on." A conversation went on in the background that Jane couldn't quite hear, then Phyllis came back on. "Where are you? Get over here."

"I'll be there as quick as I can." She turned on the car motor and edged into traffic, determined to spare Harry—or was it herself?—from whatever her friends might tell him about her.

But once she'd parked at the restaurant, she didn't want to go in. She sat in the car, getting hotter by the moment, gathering her courage. But go she must. These were the people who had gathered to mourn her (probable) murder, the people who loved her the most.

"Look what the cat dragged in," Phyllis observed when Jane, slightly breathless, found them. The remains of lunch still sat on the table. Harry was eating a burger.

"Not dragged." Jane smiled pleasantly. "I came of my own volition."

They all turned to look at her. Harry looked curious, Helen worried, Phyllis annoyed. Irma spoke first. "Where were you?"

"I wish I had a more dramatic story to tell." Jane squeezed into the booth. "Remember the photo of the car I showed Detective Alvarez this morning?"

"We're all up on that part of the story," Irma assured her.

"I spotted the SUV on the drive over here, and I just had to confirm it was the same one."

Helen looked at the watch on her thin wrist, an exaggerated movement. "That couldn't have taken this long."

"The SUV belongs to Clark Kinnon, the guy who flipped Megan's house. So naturally, I had to talk to him."

No one said anything for a moment.

"You what?" Irma broke the silence.

Helen cleared her throat. "Jane, I realize you became

entangled in that terrible murder at Walden Spring last year, but you're not going to make this a habit, are you?"

"No one has said Megan is dead." Jane was surprised by her vehemence.

"You know that's not what I meant." Helen looked at Harry as if willing him to speak. If anyone could put an end to this madness, it was he. He was her boyfriend, and he had also been in law enforcement, somehow, though they were all pretty hazy on exactly how.

But Harry was too smart to fall into that trap. He rose. "As long as you're okay, I'll leave you to your lunch." He kissed her cheek.

But it was too late, and Jane wasn't hungry. She piled Phyllis and Helen into her car while Harry drove Irma home. He showed up about twenty minutes after Jane let herself into her house. Irma must have chewed his ear off.

"We need to talk about what happened today," he said.

"No, we don't." Jane smiled to lighten the mood and reassure him.

"You realize you could have cornered a killer today. Does that seem smart to you?"

"I didn't. I cornered a philanderer. I'm fine now, and I've avoided distracting the police with another stupid lead."

"I heard about the home search from your friends." Harry's mouth was a thin line under his thick mustache. "Look, I'm not going to tell you what to do. I'm not going to tell you how to do your job." He cleared his throat and lowered his voice. "But I am going to tell you that if something happened to you, I don't know how I would survive it. We're at an age where every moment is precious, and every moment is increasingly precarious. I could handle it if you got sick. I've lived through that before. But if you were killed or severely injured in some foolish and avoidable situation, I don't know what I would do. I love you."

Astonished, Jane looked up at Harry and then down at her feet. It had been a long time since anyone had declared his love for her. Decades. Not through the arid final years of her marriage. Not from her son. Her eyes stung. She moved toward Harry, who enveloped her in his arms.

"I love you too," she said.

"It's not just you anymore," he whispered. "You need to be more careful." And then he kissed her.

Chapter Forty-two

Harry was out picking up Chinese food for dinner when Jane's phone rang. She was in her kitchen, her head in the refrigerator looking for an open bottle of wine. The phone was in her handbag, which was on the counter. She dug it out in time to see the name LAURA REEVE right before the screen went dark.

"*Drat!*" She pressed the button to call back.

"Jane? Is that you?"

"It is. Sorry I missed your call. My cell phone was in the bottom of my bag."

Laura laughed appreciatively. "Yet another reason to be glad I don't have one."

Neither of them said anything for a moment. Finally, Jane spoke up. "Thank you so much for agreeing to see Maggie and me at your house on Tuesday," Jane said. "I was sorry to intrude, especially with such unhappy news."

"You haven't heard anything?"

"I would have called you immediately. Or the police would have. I know you reached out to Detective Alvarez."

"Yes. Thank you for making it happen." There was a catch in Laura's voice, and the phone went silent again while she fought for control. "I am so sorry to call you." Laura was crying now. "I didn't know who to talk to. Poor Maggie has so much on her plate. I didn't want to add my troubles to hers any more than I already do."

"It's okay. I'm here." Jane found her way to her darkening living room and sat down in her chair.

Laura was still crying. Jane waited, keeping her breath even so no sound would travel down the line.

"I'm sorry." Laura blew her nose.

"Don't be."

"I'm so scared. And I miss Megan so much. How can I miss someone so much I haven't seen in seven years?"

"I haven't seen my son in almost eleven years," Jane said. The words were difficult. It wasn't a topic Jane raised with strangers. It had been torturous even to tell Harry about it, and he certainly deserved to know.

"Oh!" Laura sounded surprised. Estrangement from one's children wasn't a common condition. "Is he—"

"He's alive," Jane said. "And living in San Francisco."

"And why do you not—?"

"I wish I could say I knew why," Jane answered, though she did, of course, have inklings. Ideas that had formed on sleepless nights.

"I wish I didn't know why," Laura said. "But I know all too well." She drew a sharp breath and began. "I was never a strong person. My brother was my parents' favorite, particularly my father's, and after my mother died, all balance was lost. It's funny really, how my father groomed my brother to be a banker or a lawyer and he ended up as the weed-smoking proprietor of a glass sculpture shop. My father must be twirling in his grave."

When she spoke again, her voice was steadier. "No one had any ambitions for me, and I had none for myself. I did okay in college, which is a good place for dreamy, introspective teenagers, but I was utterly lost when I got out. Daddy introduced me to Edwin, and he took an immediate interest in me. He was older, a successful attorney, which is how Daddy knew him. His firm represented the business. Edwin knew exactly what he wanted out of life, and it was the path of least resistance to have his vision of the future become mine as well."

"It's so easy to adopt someone else's certainty as our own," Jane commented.

"Isn't it? Anyway, we married, bought a house in Cambridge. Megan came along in less than a year. I see now how overwhelmed I was, caring for a baby, alone in the house all day. I should have asked Edwin if I could hire some help. Or I should have gone out more. They have all those mothers' groups now. Maybe they had them then. I didn't think to look. I was ashamed I couldn't handle it and determined to keep it all together on my own."

The thought of Laura Reeve, alone, in a big cold house with a baby was depressing. Surely everyone who knew her—her husband, father, brother—should have realized she was struggling. But apparently no one did.

"It was never a happy marriage," Laura was saying, "though I suppose I had no basis to compare it. Edwin wanted a sparkling younger woman to have on his arm and make conversation with clients and friends. Perhaps he thought I'd grow into the role or I could will myself to do it, but neither was true. He started staying out in the evenings, either at work or doing the social part of his job, which became more demanding when he became a partner. That made my lonely days even longer.

"I understand now it wasn't his fault, though it's taken a lot of therapy to get there. I was an adult. I could have done something, but instead I slid down and down. I never made an effort to make friends in Cambridge. Never called on old college or high school friends, though I knew there were some in the area. Never joined a church, never volunteered, never took a class. It was easy to use my baby as an excuse, but it was my failing. I became dull and a hopeless screwup, and Edwin left me for another woman who was much more interesting."

Laura could have been describing Jane's life, though Jane had never been without ambition. The question had been why she'd been willing to subvert it to the role her husband's job defined, the role of faculty wife, for so long. But when Francis had left her, Jane had been saved by the bridge group, who had sat with her, cried with her, made her laugh, and helped her figure out how to dig her way out of the debt he left behind. Like Laura, Jane had been left by herself with a child, but she hadn't been alone.

"We didn't divorce right away," Laura said. "His lady friend was also married, so she needed to disentangle. Edwin took an apartment on Beacon Hill, and I stayed in the house in Cambridge. He was always a good father. Even after he moved out, he came and went as he wanted.

"When Megan went off to kindergarten, I began to drink, in the mornings, when she was gone. I had always found comfort in alcohol, and looking back both my parents were probably alcoholics, though I didn't see it at the time. And certainly the voracity with which my brother attacked drug-taking should have been a warning. All I know is, less than six months earlier, the idea of drinking in the morning would have shocked me, but by the time I started, it seemed like the most obvious thing to do in the world.

"The drinking was bad, though not as bad as it would get, but then my mental health started to slip. Packages started showing up at the house, dozens of them, addressed to me and charged to a credit card Edwin paid. They were all things I liked, clothes and household goods, but I couldn't remember ordering any of them. I didn't know what blackouts were then.

"The bills prompted Edwin to sue for divorce, so there would be a formal financial arrangement and he'd no longer be responsible for my debts. That resulted in a court-approved custody arrangement too. He had Megan Wednesday nights and weekends. Ellen had moved into his apartment by then. She was divorced, too, and they married soon after."

"Andy Bromfield told me Megan had a stepmother."

"Ellen was a good person. She raised my daughter well."

They were both silent for a moment, then Laura picked up the tale. "Once we were divorced, and I was drinking, things started going very wrong. I couldn't manage the household. Food would rot in the refrigerator, stuff I couldn't even remember buying. I tried so hard, but I would forget to pick up Megan in the afternoons, stranding her at ballet or scouts. I put an erasable calendar up on the refrigerator and made a schedule every week, but somehow I still missed stuff, and then I would get these calls wondering where I was. When we'd get home I would check and the appointment would be right there on the schedule, clear as day. In my befuddled state, I hadn't seen it. Or hadn't understood what it said. Or something. The other parents were so helpful, covering for me, but they began to question my fitness, as well they should have.

"One day I got a call from the school. Megan was terribly sick, and I needed to pick her up. When I got there, Megan was in the bathroom in the nurse's office, vomiting. The school nurse held out a plastic baggie containing a turkey sandwich, the one I'd packed in Megan's lunch that morning. The meat was blue with mold and smelled disgusting. Megan had eaten a few bites. She was such an obedient child. But then she'd burst into tears in the lunchroom, and one of the teachers brought her to the nurse's office along with the remains of the sandwich.

"The nurse could tell I'd been drinking. She'd already called Edwin. He stormed in from his office and took Megan to his apartment. He went back to court and got full custody on the basis that I was unfit. The day after the hearing, my brother took me to rehab for the first time."

In her fully dark living room, with the glow of her cell phone surrounding her chin and cheek, Jane wished this conversation had taken place in person. She could have made some gesture of encouragement, leaned across and patted Laura's hand. But to say something aloud, she judged, might end the call.

Finally, Laura found the courage to go on. When she spoke, the words rushed out of her. "I intended to work to regain custody. I vowed I would fight to get my daughter back. When I saw her during my periods of sobriety, I promised we would live together again. But I could never keep it together long enough to get through any sort of court process. By high school I'd given up promising Megan she could live with me. She was happy at Edwin and Ellen's house. It was her home." Laura began to cry again, but she kept talking. "I never saw her room, never even saw photos of it, but I pictured it with posters of bands on the walls and stuffed animals on the bed. We met in coffee shops on Beacon Hill where she lived or in Cambridge near her school. I was always uncomfortable there. I had never adapted to the city. I promised her instead of living together we'd go on fabulous vacations, or outings. But those didn't happen either.

"When Megan graduated from law school, she told me she didn't want to see me anymore. Studying for the bar was all-consuming and she couldn't deal with it and deal with me, emotionally. I understood, I really did. There had been so many broken promises, so many disappointments. Megan told me every time she watched me drive away that she worried I would die from drunk driving or alcohol poisoning or my body would give out. She couldn't do it anymore.

"I acquiesced. Staying away was the one thing I could do right for my daughter." A ragged sob came through Jane's phone. "But I always believed . . ." Laura sobbed again. "I always believed I would see my baby again. I dreamed I would dance at her wedding and sing to her children. I never, ever let myself believe it was really the end."

"It isn't the end," Jane said with more conviction than she felt, because this woman needed to hold on to hope for a few more days or hours, however long it took until the call from Detective Alvarez inevitably came.

"Thank you for caring about my Megan." Laura choked the words out.

"It isn't the end," Jane repeated. She needed to believe it herself.

Chapter Forty-three

After they hung up, Jane sat in her living room, not bothering to turn on the lights, mulling the conversation in her mind.

"I'm here!" Harry came through the kitchen door. Jane heard him pulling out plates to serve the Chinese food.

"I'll be there in a sec." Jane's stomach growled. She'd missed breakfast and lunch, but she continued to sit in her pink chair, thinking about her conversation with Laura Reeve. Laura took responsibility for her failings as a mother. For isolating herself, for the drinking, and the resulting chaos. She described her mental health as precarious, and that was no doubt true.

But the mother's experience had eerie parallels to the daughter's. The mother received packages in the mail, goods she didn't remember ordering. The daughter woke up in the night bathed in sweat. The mother found rotting food in her refrigerator. The daughter saw flashing lights through her eyelids that disappeared when she opened her eyes. The mother missed appointments and then returned home to see them clearly marked on her calendar. The daughter lost time in the night; hours sped by like minutes.

Both women had been subjected to gaslighting, using the technology of their particular eras. Jane rocked back in her chair when she realized it.

The women had responded differently to their predicaments. Laura had fallen apart, taken to drink, and lost her child. Megan had doubled down, excelling at work and planning her future. Both women had questioned their sanity.

There was only one person who connected the two women. Laura had been the young wife, the woman who didn't know her mind, who didn't have a vision for her life. But Megan was like her father, strong and successful at work. It hadn't been so easy to break her.

The cell phone was still in Jane's hand. She called Detective Alvarez.

He picked right up, talking at a fast clip. "Jane. Saw it was you. I only have a minute."

"Sorry to call so late. It's important. I know who was gaslighting Megan."

He didn't ask who. "So do I. The technology guys at the state police figured out whose phone was used to harass her. We got the call an hour ago. There are other indications of motive, too. We have an arrest warrant. We're on our way to pick him up."

"Edwin Larsen." They said it simultaneously.

"How did you know?" Alvarez asked.

"It's complicated. I'll tell you later." Jane hesitated. "He'll have a good lawyer."

"I know. We're close. Got to go."

Jane said good-bye and went to the kitchen to share the news with Harry. An arrest. An arrest was imminent. At last.

Chapter Forty-four

The next morning Jane entered the Middlesex County jail, accompanied by Vernon Thrush, Edwin Larsen's defense attorney. Edwin had asked to see her.

She'd been astonished by the call. Thrush had explained that Edwin was asking for her, and police and prison officials had given her permission to see him. Why would Edwin ask to see her? For a split second Jane wondered if perhaps he wanted to ask her to take care of his daughter's cat. She dismissed the idea as quickly as it came to her. Edwin Larsen didn't care about the cat.

Thrush, a sturdily built man in late middle age, knew the drill well. He handed over his briefcase for inspection and fished his keys, phone, and wallet out of his pockets before he went through the metal detector. Jane followed his lead, wishing she had cleaned out her pocketbook before heading to the jail, but there hadn't been time.

Edwin was already seated at a beat-up table with shiny

metal legs and a dull green top when they entered. Jane wondered if he was restrained in some way, which led her to speculate about what he'd been charged with. Was it the abduction and disappearance of his daughter? Or was it a lesser charge having to do with the online harassment? But in that case, why hadn't he made bail? She'd called Alvarez right after Vernon Thrush had invited her to the jail, but the detective hadn't gotten back to her yet.

Edwin looked up when he heard the door open, and Vernon and Jane entered the room. His eyes were red-rimmed with bags so large beneath them it looked painful. He was dressed in a prison jumpsuit that showed his pale lower arms, covered in gray hairs. Not nearly so impressive as when they were covered by his blue pinstriped suit jacket, with the French cuffs with the fancy cuff links poking out.

Thrush sat on the same side of the table as Jane, which surprised her. Somehow she'd expected him to sit next to his client. But Jane wasn't there to interrogate Edwin. She wasn't sure why she was there.

Edwin wasted no time with small talk. His bright blue eyes met hers. "I didn't take my daughter. I don't know where she is. They think if they keep asking me over and over, I'll break down and tell them what I did with her. The problem is, I didn't do anything."

A surprising statement. It took Jane a moment to understand what it meant. "But you did use her security system to harass her. Just like you changed the dates on the calendar, put rotting food in the refrigerator, and mail-ordered expensive items to harass her mother."

Edwin had opened his mouth to speak, but he abruptly shut it.

Vernon Thrush spoke up. "Mr. Larsen is not going to

answer questions about the alleged gaslighting of his daughter. His concern is for her well-being."

Jane leaned forward, folding her arms on the hard surface of the table. "Why did you ask for me?"

"You started all this talk about the gaslighting. I was there that first morning when you mentioned it to the detective. You pointed the police in this direction. But it's the wrong direction. Now you need to fix it. I can't convince them I didn't take her, but I may be able to convince you. And you, in turn, may be able to convince them. I've seen your influence."

Jane wasn't so sure about that influence, especially after she'd sent the police on a fruitless chase through the empty houses in her neighborhood. "It's hard to believe that one person was harassing Megan and a different person is responsible for her disappearance."

Edwin rubbed his red-rimmed eyes. "I know it is. But you have to believe me."

It was all too much for Jane to take in. The jail setting. The idea that a father would do what he stood accused of doing. Did he harass the women in his life for the pleasure of it, or was there a purpose to it, some personal gain? With Laura, the harassment had freed him to marry a second time and to have sole custody of his daughter. Jane felt strongly there must be some similar motive here; his actions must have been driven by greed or need. "But why? Why would you gaslight your daughter?"

Edwin glanced at his lawyer, who shook his head in one quick motion that said emphatically, "No."

"I can't talk to you about that," Edwin said. "I can only say, if I did it, I had my reasons and they are unique reasons. No one else would have the same motive."

"If you didn't take Megan, why in the beginning did

you discourage the police from investigating? As her father, you should have been frantic."

"That is my great shame now that I did that. I knew if the police investigated there would be . . . er . . . *complications* for me. And, you truly must believe me, in the beginning I really thought Megan had run away from her life and was hiding out somewhere. She would come back in her own time."

Ran away because of the stress you deliberately caused. The man was clearly a psychopath. But strangely, Jane believed him. He didn't have Megan or know where she was. Though certainly his motive in convincing Jane of this was to save his own skin, not to save his daughter.

She didn't want to help him, but she did want to help Megan any way she could. "I'm not sure what you're proposing I do."

"Your energy and influence propelled the police in my direction. I'm now asking that you send them in some other direction. Specifically, in the direction of Megan."

"If I knew who took her, I would have told the police when this all began."

"There must have been other people on your suspect list. If it's not me, it's likely to be one of them. Get the police to give up their fixation on me and move on. Megan's life may depend on it."

Megan was most likely already dead. Logic told Jane that. It had been nine days and not a word from her. But Jane's heart battled to overrule her head. She desperately wanted Megan to be alive.

Chapter Forty-five

"What did he want?" Jane and Alvarez were in the small conference room down the hall from his desk at Cambridge police headquarters. He was seated across from her, and though he'd offered coffee, each had settled for a glass of water, tepid—the way it came out of the so-called cooler.

"He wanted to convince me he didn't take Megan and he doesn't know where she is."

"What a load." Alvarez sat back in the hard chair. "The guy's a stone-cold psychopath if you ask me, to do that to his own kid." He shifted forward again, putting his arms on the table. "You haven't told me how you figured out it was him."

Jane told him about the parallels to Laura Reeve's life. Despite all he'd seen and heard during his life as a cop, as Jane described the gaslighting of Megan's mother, Alvarez's big brown eyes grew wider. "He is one sick guy."

"He is, but I think he's telling the truth about Megan. He harassed her, but he doesn't have her. Both things can be true."

"Jane, you're the one who insisted from the beginning the two things must be related. The analysis of the phone data is incontrovertible. Larsen was the one who was in Megan's home security system. He turned up the thermostat, advanced the digital clock on the cable system, flashed the lights, played recordings of voices, all in an attempt to make his own daughter think she was crazy. He played on an insecurity she already had—the belief that her mother had major mental health issues. Now you sit here telling me he did the same thing to her mother thirty years ago. Surely you can see how damning this all is."

"*Why* did he do it? What did he have to gain?"

"That one's easy. He'd stolen from Megan's trust and he was about to be found out." Alvarez smiled triumphantly. Jane realized he'd been sitting on this gem, waiting for her to ask.

Her reaction must have satisfied him. "What!"

"He walks around like he's still a big shot lawyer, but his firm has been circling the drain for years. He's been putting money into it, not taking money out. He's burned more than one client with bad advice or careless lawyering. He's a great one for getting his name in the paper, but he's more interested in holding the spotlight than doing what's right for his clients. Boston is a small city, and word gets around. He had an expensive lifestyle to maintain. Megan's trust must have been too tempting."

It all made sense. The rows of empty offices in Franklin and Larsen's expensive piece of Boston real estate. What Andy had said about no one from his year at Harvard being asked to join the firm. Associates made money for the firm by billing hours to clients. A failing partnership wouldn't want associates sitting around with no one to bill hours to.

"And Megan was about to ask him for half a million dollars to buy into the partnership at her law firm," Jane said.

Alvarez whistled. "He wouldn't have been able to give it to her. In any case, she turns thirty-five in November. The trust goes to her control. We have forensic accountants looking at it, but I took a quick look and even I could see it." Alvarez had worked in Fraud before he moved to Major Crimes. "With her training, it would have taken Megan seconds to figure out she'd been robbed and who must have done it. He had motive. And he's all but confessed to the harassment. Now we need him to tell us where she is. We've searched his home. We're in the process of going through the information on his computer and phone. He has a summer house on Cape Cod. We've searched that as well."

"Do you believe she's alive?" Jane felt a spark of hope.

"I don't know," Alvarez said. "I want to believe a father would be less likely than a stranger to kill his daughter, but I know better."

Jane thought for a moment. "But abducting her and holding her doesn't help him if you're right about the motive. When she returns, sooner or later, the money will still be missing from the trust."

"Unless he had some scheme to return the money, you're right," Alvarez conceded. "Otherwise only killing her covers up his crime."

"Or . . ." Jane was eager to offer an alternative. "If he convinced Megan she was crazy so she would voluntarily ask him to continue to manage her money, or, failing that, he goes to the court and forces the issue by having her declared incompetent. In neither case is it part of the plan or necessary to abduct her or kill her. Maybe Edwin Larsen is telling the truth. He didn't take her."

"Maybe," Alvarez responded, admitting the possibility but sounding far from convinced.

"Why did the district attorney agree to let him see me?" Jane asked.

"We thought you might get something from him we wouldn't. Larsen asked for you specifically. You knew his daughter. Honestly, I thought he might confess."

"I don't think his attorney would have let him, even if he'd had a mind to. Which he didn't." Jane hesitated. "One thing that I don't understand. Edwin Larsen had the ability to use the security system to gaslight Megan. Anyone with access to the app and her codes could have done that. But what about the logs for the night she was taken? Could he have removed all traces of her leaving? That seems like a much more technologically sophisticated activity. Is there any indication Edwin Larsen had the necessary level of skill?" Jane doubted it very much. Not to indulge in stereotypes, but why would a sixty-something lawyer have the ability to hack into the system at Acme Security?

"You said it yourself," Alvarez reminded her. "What are the odds two people were in that system?"

"So you're not looking for anyone else?"

"We're looking for Megan, of course. Finding her, dead or alive, is our highest priority. But as for suspects, we're concentrating on landing the fish we have on the hook. Not trawling the whole wide ocean."

Jane left Cambridge police headquarters and drove home, steering the Volvo through the crowded streets. She couldn't remember being more discouraged. Megan had been gone for so long, it seemed unlikely she would ever be back. Her father was an odious man. Jane understood why Andy had said Megan was raised by wolves. Edwin Larsen's only motivation in talking to Jane was an attempt to save his own skin.

And yet.

And yet.

Jane believed him.

Chapter Forty-six

At home, Jane paced from her study to the kitchen, through the dining room to the living room and back again.

Against all odds, she believed Edwin Larsen. He had gaslit his daughter using her home security system. He had tried to convince her she was crazy, and almost succeeded. He had lied, covered up, and tried to divert the police when his daughter had disappeared. He was an odious man.

But he didn't have her. He hadn't taken her.

The confounding thing was the logs of the security system. If one accepted the premise that Larsen didn't have the skills to have altered them, the people involved in the case who did were Howard Borg—Megan's creepy online date who ran a cybersecurity company—and someone at Acme.

Jane itched to act. The only thing to do was to begin at the beginning. The beginning with Howard, for Jane and for Megan, had been at Peet's in Harvard Square. Jane grabbed her pocketbook and headed out the door.

She was happy to see Tonya, the tiny barista, behind the counter. "Hi, Jane. Usual?"

"Iced, I think. It's still awfully warm."

"It is. I wish it would cool off already. I'm sick of my summer clothes. Can't wait to switch them out."

Jane didn't want to think about her closet or the task of cleaning out clothes. "Tonya, the last time I was here, I met Howard Borg, remember? You said he came in quite often."

"Yeah. I remember. Yuck."

"I need some information about him. Things he might have said to you or one of your coworkers, or that one of you overheard when he spoke to his coffee dates."

Tonya handed Jane her iced coffee and called out, "I'm taking my break!"

They moved to a table. Tonya sat back against the hard seat, designed to make patrons comfortable but not for too long. "We all know him. He's here almost every other day with a different woman. He finds them online. Whenever I see a woman who fits his type sitting and waiting, I always want to tell her to run. Although I never have. When they walk out, and they always do, he hangs around and hits on us. Everyone knows to look out for him and rescue whoever he's talking to."

Jane sat back, too, mirroring Tonya's relaxed posture. She suspected talking about this outrageous guy was fun but actually dealing with him, not so much. "I get that he creeps everyone out by hitting on them, but what specifically makes him so creepy?"

"He comes on way too strong, for one thing. He doesn't chat with you and then maybe ask you out for a drink. He jumps right to asking you to his house, or to go away for the weekend, or even to travel with him. He tells you what a hotshot he is, how great his apartment is, all his glamorous trips. That's a part of his sales technique, but really, it makes you want to run."

Jane was having trouble keeping up with the torrent of words. Tonya had a lot of feelings about Howard Borg. "He asked you away for the weekend?"

"Many times."

"Did he say where?"

"Different places. Cape Cod. He said he had a cabin in the White Mountains. Paris, one time even."

"He said he owned a cabin in New Hampshire?"

"In the woods. I think he meant it to be romantic, but the idea of it, of being alone with him, creeped me out more than anything else he said. Finally, our manager told him that baristas aren't allowed to talk to customers. Which is ridiculous, because we obviously talk to customers all day long. It's the best part of the job. Like you and Harry. I love talking to you guys. But that guy is too much. He wouldn't give up. Some of the younger girls were really scared of him."

"When he asked you to New Hampshire, did he happen to mention where this cabin was?"

"If he did, I wasn't listening. An isolated cabin in the woods." She hugged herself. "It seemed strange, because he doesn't come off like an outdoorsy type, but so much else about him was strange, you know?"

Behind the counter the manager signaled to Tonya to speed it up.

"I gotta go back. Sorry. I can't think where his cabin was. Do you want me to ask around? Will it help your client?"

Jane handed Tonya a PROFESSIONAL BUSYBODY card, not the first she had given her. Tonya slipped it into her apron pocket. "I think it could help my client very much indeed," Jane told her.

Chapter Forty-seven

Jane drove straight to Acme Security.

"You again," Agnes said as Jane came through the door.

"Me again," Jane agreed. "The last time I was here, I asked to speak to your technician, Justin Vreeland. Did you give him my message?"

"I did indeed. Did he call you?" There was no hesitation when she said it. Despite Jane's skepticism, she had done her bit in the message chain and that was it. Which meant Justin hadn't told Agnes that Jane had visited his home, because surely his wife had told him. Which seemed odd. But perhaps he didn't come to the office that often, loading up his van infrequently and taking it straight to the job site from home. Maybe his relationship with Agnes, his boss, was transactional, one of phone calls and texts, orders given and received. Maybe they weren't friends in any sense. Jane didn't puzzle about it long; she had come on a more pressing issue.

"When we spoke about someone hacking or breaking into the security system at Megan Larsen's house, you told me it would be easy if that person had the app and the codes. But what about the system logs? Could someone from the outside access them?"

"Absolutely not." Agnes sniffed. "And I never told you it would be 'easy' to hack into one of our security systems. I told you that some humans are careless with their codes."

"You're right." Jane smiled. "I apologize. Have the police told you that the logs for Megan Larsen's system show no one entering or exiting her house on the night she disappeared?"

Agnes's mouth opened. Then she thought better of whatever she'd been going to say and snapped it shut. Jane felt a twinge of worry. Head down, determined to follow her own path, she'd clearly overstepped.

"They're wrong," Agnes declared. "While someone with bad intent, with the app and the codes, could manipulate things in a home using the security system, no one—absolutely no one—can get inside it."

"You seem certain."

"I am. The vendors we deal with test their systems thoroughly, and we test every system independently after we install it."

"Is that something your employees do?" The office held no desks or equipment for computer types. Was this part of what Justin did at home at night, the work his wife had complained about?

"No. We can't have our own people do the testing.

That would invalidate it. We contract with an outside firm to certify the work."

Jane's heart beat a little faster. "What is the name of that firm?"

That slowed Agnes down. "Why do you want to know? I told you, the police have been here. I've given them everything I can. Besides, didn't I hear on the radio on the drive into work today there had been an arrest?"

Jane's phone buzzed inside her pocketbook. She left it where it was. "There has been an arrest. The police are busy with that. I'm tidying up a few things for my own interest. Did the police ask about your outside testing firm?"

"No."

"So it's not of interest to them. Only me. Will you tell me?"

Jane's phone buzzed again, and Agnes's phone rang too. She picked it up. "Hold please." She looked at Jane. "Will you go away if I tell you?"

"Happily."

"Lockdown Cybersecurity Limited."

Howard Borg's firm.

Chapter Forty-eight

In her car in front of Acme, Jane pulled her cell phone out of her pocketbook. Her heart thumped, banging with adrenaline, and her hands shook a little. The call that had come in while she was talking to Agnes was from an unknown 617 number. Whoever it was had called twice and then left a voice mail. Jane played the recording.

"Jane! It's Tonya. I was about to leave for the day when my friend Leah came on shift. She's had more than her share of encounters with weird Howard, so I asked if she knew where his cabin was. She remembered! She has friends who vacation in the same town, so the name was familiar. Anyway, she's pretty sure Howard's cabin is in Madison, New Hampshire."

Saying a silent thank-you to Tonya, Jane called Detective Alvarez. He picked up right away.

"Where are you?" Jane asked.

"At my desk talking to you."

"Anything from Larsen yet?"

Alvarez exhaled noisily. "The guy is saying nothing, except begging us over and over to look for his daughter. His lawyer is a pain in my rear. Our hope is that if Larsen has her somewhere and was taking her food and water, he'll realize she's in danger of dying of thirst or starvation and tell us where she is."

"Is that likely? You said he was a psychopath."

"We've charged him on the financial crimes, and we'll see if we can hold him long enough to make him panic. It will be tricky. He'll certainly make bail, but maybe we can slow-walk this into the weekend. Megan is his daughter. He does seem to care about her."

"He cares more about her as a prize in a custody fight or an accomplished Harvard lawyer he can brag about than he does as a human being."

"True, but he's our best hope."

"Maybe not. I'm calling to offer you an alternative."

"Jane, we've been over this."

"Hear me out." Jane paused to gather her thoughts. She was confident in her powers of persuasion with Alvarez, but success depended on approaching him the right way. "I'm still bothered by the idea that Larsen wouldn't have had the skills to erase all traces of his entry into the house and Megan's exit on the night she was taken."

"We've talked about this."

"We have, but when you talked to him, did Howard Borg tell you he has a contract with Acme Security to test the systems they install? He gets *paid* to hack into Acme systems." Jane stopped talking, hoping the import of her message was sinking in.

Alvarez responded after a moment. "No. I wouldn't, honestly, have thought to ask him about Acme directly. At the time I was interviewing him about a bad coffee date he had with Megan."

"That's what I thought too," Jane said. "But there's more. I spoke to one of the baristas at Peet's, which is where Howard met up with Megan and with many other women, several a week. The barista told me that all the women who work there are wary of him. He comes on strong and repeatedly. One thing he's offered many of them? A weekend alone with him in his cabin in the woods in Madison, New Hampshire."

Alvarez swore and then went quiet, no doubt thinking through the case, thinking about what he had to do next. "We have to check that cabin out. Did she give you an address?"

"Just the town."

"We'll ask the New Hampshire State Police for assistance."

"Keep in touch."

"You'll be the first person I call if anything happens. Or the second. Or third." He made a half-grunt, half-laugh. "You'll definitely be in my first half dozen calls. I've got to go. I want to get on this while we still have daylight."

Chapter Forty-nine

When they ended the call, Jane drove home. Once there, she couldn't settle. Could they really, finally, be on the verge of finding Megan? And when they found her, would she be alive or dead?

Jane needed someone to wait with her. If they were available, Helen, Phyllis, or Irma would be with her in a flash, with quivers full of interesting topics in an attempt to distract her. Harry would have sensible advice about waiting until she heard something concrete, which wouldn't be helpful. If she could have done that, she would have. She needed someone who cared as much about the investigation as she did. Jane wanted to call Laura Reeve but couldn't raise that much hope in the poor woman until they were certain. The call to Laura was Alvarez's to make, for good or for ill.

Jane picked her phone up off the kitchen counter and

dialed Andy Bromfield. Alvarez had been suspicious of him, but surely with Edwin Larsen having all but confessed to the gaslighting and the police in pursuit of Howard Borg, Andy could no longer be considered a suspect.

Andy answered immediately, and when she described to him in big, broad strokes what was happening, he shouted, "I'll be right over!"

Twenty minutes later Andy knocked on her front door. He'd parked in Megan's driveway, obviously in great haste, his car left at an odd angle.

"Anything?" he asked, breathless, when Jane opened the door.

"No, but I wouldn't expect anything yet." She didn't tell him she'd spent the time until he got there refreshing her web browser looking for headlines.

"Tell me what's happening. They arrested Megan's father. Where did this new lead come from? Why New Hampshire? Does Edwin own property there?"

"I met with Edwin Larsen at the jail at his request." Jane spoke slowly, giving Andy time to absorb. "He told me he didn't take Megan."

"I knew it!" Andy shouted. "As soon as I heard the news, I said, 'No. That's not it.'"

"Why didn't you think it was him? You certainly dislike him."

Andy wrinkled his brow, considering. "It's not his style. He doesn't get his hands dirty. He's a man-behind-the-curtain type. If he's responsible, he had someone else take her."

The gaslighting of both Laura and Megan had been the acts of an invisible force, the man behind the curtain.

"Do you think that's what happened?" Andy asked.

"He had someone take her and then it went wrong some-how?"

They were seated in Jane's living room, the place they'd landed when Andy had charged through Jane's front door. "The property the police are searching belongs to some-one Megan went on an online date with," Jane said. "He has no connection to Edwin Larsen."

"An online date?" Andy didn't hide his surprise. "She never told me." They hadn't been as close as Andy had believed.

"Megan is good at compartmentalizing," Jane said, hoping to make him feel better. "Probably a survival technique left over from her childhood."

Jane explained in more detail about Howard Borg and how he'd come to be a suspect. Then they fell silent, picking up their phones looking for news.

Jane turned on the lights. Harry called to check in, and Phyllis called to chat. Both times Jane's phone buzzed, she and Andy jumped. Heart thumping, Jane held her breath until she saw the name on the screen.

"I'm here with Andy Bromfield," she told Harry. "I want to stay off the phone. I'll explain later."

"Are you all right?" She'd alarmed him.

"Perfectly fine, just distracted and needing to get off the phone."

"Say *codswallop* if you're really fine," Harry insisted.

"Codswallop. I've got to go. Love you." Jane blushed. She'd never said the words to him in front of an audience.

"Love you, too," Harry said, and was gone.

"What?" Andy asked.

"Nothing," Jane said.

Phyllis was more easily dispensed with. "I have com-pany," Jane told her.

"Then why did you answer?"

"Because the last time I didn't answer, you tattled to my boyfriend and threatened to call the police."

"I'll let you go." Phyllis ended the call before Jane could.

Jane returned her attention to Andy. He looked so discouraged, scrunched up on her couch, squinting through his glasses at his phone. "You've been a good friend to Megan," she said.

"I hope so. She really doesn't have any family, as you've seen. But I can't help thinking I could have been a better friend. Why didn't she tell me she was worried about her mental health? Why come to you, a stranger?"

"I don't know. Perhaps, with her mother's history, she wanted to keep her suspicions out of the mainstream of her life."

Andy grunted, showing his disagreement, though whether he disagreed with Megan's withholding her concerns or with Jane's theory about why, she couldn't tell.

The hours crawled by. Finally, after nine o'clock, Alvarez called. "She's not here."

Jane felt the air whoosh out of her lungs. "There's no sign of her? She's never been there?"

"What, what, what?" Andy was frantic. Jane put her phone on speaker.

"The New Hampshire guys got here in daylight." Alvarez's voice buzzed through the phone. "They say from the state of the driveway, no one's been here in months. The nearest neighbors can't see the place except when the leaves are down. There's not many houses nearby, and most of them are weekend places. The few people we've been able to talk to confirm that Borg hasn't been seen around town all summer. We finally got a warrant. Went in the house. No one's there."

Jane struggled not to show her disappointment for Andy's sake. "I really thought this was it."

"We have Borg at headquarters in Cambridge. We'll ask why he concealed that he worked on Ms. Larsen's security system. Megan's not here, but that doesn't mean he doesn't have her."

"I guess. Thanks for calling."

Andy swore, his voice thick with emotion. Jane thought he might cry and felt awful. She shouldn't have given him false hope, because she needed someone to sit with her while she waited.

"I'm so sorry, Andy."

And then he did cry, wiping away the tears with his sleeve. "I miss her so much, you know. And I'm scared, so scared about what's happened to her."

"I'm scared too." Jane fetched a box of tissues from her office.

Andy took one and blew his nose. "Thank you. I want her back. Even when I was at my apartment late at night, I had the comfort of knowing Megan was at her house, sitting on her couch, a half-drunk glass mug of tea on the coffee table. Knowing she was there made me happy. It made my life better."

When he'd composed himself, Jane walked Andy to the front door. "What you said about Megan, about the half-drunk cup of tea . . ."

He laughed. "It's her signature. I tease her about it all the time. At the office she'll have three half-full cups on her desk. She never finishes one, and she can't tell you why."

Jane hugged Andy, closed the door behind him, and locked it, thinking hard. Someone else had mentioned those half-drunk cups of tea. Who was it? The idea was like a ghost running from room to room as she chased it, but she couldn't catch it. She went to bed but didn't fall asleep until the night sky lightened, and she heard the unfamiliar sound of raindrops on the window.

Chapter Fifty

W hen Jane finally got out of bed, the sky was gray and a steady rain fell, bringing the loosest of the leaves, the ones from the unhealthy branches, down with it. She was puttering in her bathrobe, deflated by the failure to find Megan at Howard Borg's cabin. Her doorbell rang.

"Laura!" Megan's mother stood on the front steps, hair already dripping from the rain. A green and white cab pulled away from the curb. "Come in! Come in. You'll catch your death. How did you get here?"

Laura Reeve stepped onto the tile floor of the vestibule, took off her raincoat, and kicked off her flats. "Thanks. I'm sorry to burst in on you like this. I couldn't stop myself."

Jane took the raincoat to the kitchen and hung it over the back of a stool. It would be weeks before she would put on the heat, so the kitchen was as chilly and gray as the day outside. "Let me give you something warm to drink. Coffee? Tea?"

"Yes, tea, please." Laura watched her as Jane put the mug with a tea bag in it into the microwave, the best she could do at short notice. They were both settled at the island, Jane with coffee, before Laura spoke.

"I couldn't wait out in the Berkshires with so much going on here, the search for Megan, Edwin's arrest." She waved her hand indicating it all. "I took the first bus this morning. I was headed to the police station, to that nice Detective Alvarez, but then I thought, 'I'll be in the way there. I'll go to Jane.' Megan's house has been in the papers. I knew you lived next door. I only had to guess which house."

"That's fine," Jane reassured her. "Of course you should come here."

"Have they made any progress? Is there anything I should know?"

"Last night I thought we'd come close to finding Megan, but a promising clue came up empty." Jane told Laura the Howard Borg story. How different it sounded when she already knew the ending.

"They think Edwin has her. I can tell that from what's in the papers."

"The police think that's the most likely scenario."

Laura put down her mug and looked Jane in the eye. "But you don't."

"I went to see him at the jail." It felt like a confession. "I thought maybe I could get him to tell me something he hadn't told the police. The police thought so, too, which is why they allowed it."

"But he didn't." Laura's voice was too high and brittle, not fully in her control. The emotion she'd managed to hold back since her arrival seeped out.

"No. He didn't." Jane had her doubts about saying the rest of it. How much should this woman be asked to bear? But she pushed on. "Not only did he not tell me where Megan is, he convinced me he didn't take her."

Laura stared into the bottom of her empty cup. "I don't believe he took her either." Laura looked up at Jane. "I can believe Edwin would do many things, terrible things. But he wouldn't hurt Megan."

"He might not hurt her physically, but the police are certain of his motive. He stole from Megan's trust and then tried to convince her she was crazy."

Laura listened, gray eyes narrowed, as Jane told the story of Edwin's gaslighting. "I realized it must be him when you described what he did to you. The changing schedule, the rotting food, the mail-ordered merchandise. Same thing, different technology."

Laura had grown paler throughout the recitation, and Jane feared she might be physically sick. She swallowed loudly and then said in a shaky voice, "When it comes to money, Edwin is greedy and, for a lawyer, not at all persuaded by boundaries. He was the one who convinced my father to leave his money to Megan, with him in control in the first place, skipping over me, not even granting me a seat at the table. My own child. But I do not believe Edwin would hurt her." Laura shook her head. "Never."

Did she really believe that, or did she *need* to believe it? Jane put her hand over Laura's. "I have to get dressed. Do you mind being alone? I could call Megan's friend Andy to come over. He could wait with you."

"Andy?" Laura smiled. "I remember him. I always thought he was a nice guy."

"He is. And he and Megan have stayed friends. They work at the same firm. He's been beside himself since she disappeared. It might do you both good to spend time together."

Laura thought for a moment. "No, thanks. I'm fine on my own. I've been moving, on the bus, in the cab, in your horrendous Boston rush hour traffic this morning. It will do me good to sit still for a few minutes."

Jane went up to her room. As she rifled her closet for something warmer to wear now that the weather had finally changed, picking slacks and a long-sleeved top, she considered their conversation. Laura didn't believe Edwin had Megan, either. But then, Laura's judgment wasn't great where her ex-husband was concerned.

When Jane came back downstairs, Laura was in the living room, looking out the side window toward Megan's house, her back shaking with silent sobs.

"Laura." Jane went to her, and together they looked across Megan's puddle-filled driveway. "I am so sorry."

Laura turned to her then and put her face on Jane's shoulder. "I'm the one who is sorry. I ruined my daughter's life. I drank and acted irresponsibly. I let her father push me away when she was at the age when a daughter needs a mother most. Her memories of life with me were of instability, insecurity, lack of safety. Chaos. A child should never feel unsafe in her own home. When your childhood has been that chaotic, you never get over it."

"No, no, you misunderstand," Jane assured her. "Megan wasn't . . . isn't an unhappy person. She's accomplished a lot at a young age, and she's determined to do more. She has a real vision for her life going forward and is making it happen."

Laura had pulled away from Jane's shoulder, but her eyes ran with tears. Jane handed her a tissue from the box still on the end table from Andy's visit the night before. Her living room had been a place for grief the last twelve hours.

"When she met with me, Megan was about to move forward toward adopting a child," Jane said. "That's not something you do if you've been so scarred by your childhood you have nothing to give."

Laura looked out the window again. Wembly picked that moment, the exact right moment, to appear, winding himself around Jane's feet, meowing for his breakfast. Jane picked him up and offered him to Laura. "This is Megan's cat. She loves him. She has a lot of love to give. She isn't a miserable person."

Laura hugged the cat, pressing him to her. Wembly tolerated it, not squirming or pushing away.

Jane took the cat gently from Laura and set him on the floor. He raced her to the kitchen, where she opened a can of his fancy food. Laura followed them and watched as Jane spooned out the food and set the bowl down.

"Really," Jane said, "before all this happened, your daughter was happy." She looped her arm through Laura's. "Come on. I'll show you. You'll feel much better once you've seen Megan's house."

Chapter Fifty-one

Jane fetched two umbrellas. They didn't bother with jackets but dashed out the door and across the driveway, dodging the puddles. Jane led the way to Megan's garage door and entered the code. She pressed the button, and the door rumbled open. Laura stared, taking it all in, even though it was a mostly empty garage, before climbing the single step into the kitchen.

Laura stopped as soon as she stepped into the house, the same way Jane had the first time. Even on a dark day, the light and volume of the space were arresting. Jane took the umbrellas and set them on the concrete floor of the garage and closed the door behind them.

Jane hurried about, turning on lights. It would increase the odds of getting into trouble if a patrol car happened by, but she was anxious for Laura to see Megan's house as a warm, comfortable home.

As she bustled, Jane smelled a faint odor. A food-like odor. Was it Chinese food? She and Harry had so recently eaten it. Was she imagining the aroma?

Laura went to the living room area and stared at the painting of the lamb over the mantelpiece. "That was in my father's house when I was growing up," she said, her voice brimming with emotion. "And then in our house here in Cambridge when Megan was a girl."

"See," Jane called from the other side of the kitchen island, "she wouldn't have that here if all her memories were entirely unhappy." Jane opened the trash bin, sniffing for the Chinese food, but someone, probably the police, had long ago removed the garbage Megan had left behind. Perhaps they wanted to preserve the food to compare with Megan's stomach contents if her body was found. The recycle bin nested beside the garbage bin was still full. It gave off a slight odor of cardboard and plastic, but no food smell of any kind.

Jane hadn't smelled food the last time she was here. She tried following her nose, sniffing subtly, or she hoped subtly, so as not to raise any questions from Laura. Jane opened the refrigerator. The light went on, and the unit hummed quietly. All the perishable food had been removed, perhaps by the same unseen hand that had disposed of the garbage. The empty refrigerator had a finality about it that turned Jane's stomach. It made her feel as if Megan had gone away for a long time, probably forever. It was not the impression Jane was trying to convey to Megan's mother.

Laura had moved back over to the kitchen side of the big room. She bent slightly, held her hair away from her face, and examined the vision board. Jane went over to look at it too. The collage reflected Megan's deepest desires. Jane put her arm around Laura's shoulders. "I'll let you look around in peace." Her missing daughter's home must feel like a sacred place.

Jane walked into Megan's study. No food smells there. Jane paused in the silent room, wondering if a meal eaten days ago by the crime scene techs could have lingered, sealed in by the home's tight new windows. But it didn't seem credible. Professionals never would have eaten inside the house.

Jane opened the basement door and sniffed. The smell that wafted up to her was the smell of a dry, well-insulated basement, just as it had been when she'd been down there the last time. But was there a faint undercurrent of lo mein and kung pao chicken? She thought there was.

Jane stared at the top step. "Don't be a silly old woman," she told herself. She turned to look for Laura, who had drifted into the main part of the kitchen, where she examined the fancy coffeemaker, the dish towels, the hanging brass pans—all the things that made Megan's house a home, a place where she cooked and ate.

"I'm going downstairs to make sure there's no water coming in from this deluge." Jane kept her tone light.

Laura muttered a distracted "mmm-hmm."

Jane checked to make sure her cell phone was in the pocket of her slacks and felt reassured by its hard metal touch. She planted a foot, carefully, on the top step and made her way down the stairs.

Light filtered through the narrow basement windows. Jane followed her nose toward the wine refrigerator, then stopped short. The door to the panic room was open. Not completely, but about a foot, and even more surprising, there was a light on in the room. The smell of Chinese food was strong.

Jane pulled her phone out of her pocket as she considered the possibilities. Had Megan been hiding out in her panic room all along—just secreted somewhere else in the house on the day Jane stumbled on it? Had squatters moved into the house during the short time it had been empty? As quickly as they came to her, Jane rejected these notions. Megan couldn't have known that Jane would come into the house that particular day. And squatters would have made themselves more comfortable. They had the whole house to use.

Jane backed up three paces and pressed the number 9 on her phone.

"Hand me that. I'll get rid of the trash and then take you to the toilet before I go." A man's voice, gruff, followed by a soft female voice murmuring assent.

Jane gasped so loud she was afraid they'd heard her. Hands trembling, she pressed 1.

The door to the panic room burst open and Justin Vreeland came out, carrying a cardboard food container and an empty paper cup. He looked directly at Jane.

Jane tried to jab the second 1 to complete the 911 call but missed the digit, hitting the phone so hard with her shaky hand that it clattered onto the concrete floor.

"You!" she said.

Of course it was him. He, who spent hours every night monitoring houses with Acme systems. He, who had the skills and knowledge to erase his tracks from the system. He, who the very first time she had met him mentioned the half-drunk cups of tea on Megan's coffee table. Would he have remembered that tiny detail based on a single visit the day he came to teach her to use the security system? Or would he have noticed it as he watched her night after night from his home?

He was as shocked to see her as she had been to see him. He dropped the containers when she dropped the phone. But his shock lasted just a moment and then he came toward her, hands out, to grab, choke, strike, Jane didn't know what.

"Megan!" Jane yelled. Was Megan tied up, restrained? "Megan! LAURA!" The last word she yelled, pushing out every breath in her body to force the sound to the upstairs.

It was the last thing she got out before he fell upon her. He knocked her down and grabbed her arms. "You! I knew you were trouble. I should have done something about you when you came to my house and upset my wife."

Jane struggled mightily. He had her arms pinned against the cold floor, but she kicked out as well as she was able, hoping to find the right spot.

Her movement only made him angrier. He put his arm across her throat, choking her. She thrashed and pushed and tried to cry out, but the pressure on her throat meant she couldn't make a sound beyond a low gurgle. Her peripheral vision was fading, and she felt as if she were in a tunnel. She stared at the face of Justin Vreeland, a nose away from her, flushed red under his red beard. Would his be the last face she'd ever see?

Then *clang*! He fell across her, a heavy weight, unconscious and unmoving.

Jane looked up. Laura stood above them both, one of Megan's fancy brass cooking pans in her hands.

Laura stared openmouthed at Jane trapped under the

unconscious man. Then something else caught her attention. She turned, her breath catching as she did.

From her angle on the ground, Jane saw Megan propped against the doorframe of the panic room, barely standing, wrapped in the old crocheted afghan. "Mom!" she cried, and then she stumbled into her mother's arms.

Chapter Fifty-two

It was hours before Detective Alvarez pushed the door-bell at Jane's house. In the interim she'd been seen by the young EMT in the back of an ambulance, who'd made sure no bones were broken and advised her to take ibuprofen before she started to ache, "because for sure you're going to."

Another ambulance had left the scene with Megan, Laura, and a female detective in the back.

Vreeland was taken off in a third ambulance, re-strained to the gurney and accompanied by two uni-formed officers. He'd just begun to stir when the first officer to arrive on the scene had come vaulting down the cellar stairs.

"I don't understand. Was she there all along?" Jane asked the EMT, who raised her shoulders in the "who knows" gesture. How could she possibly know?

Jane asked the officer who took her preliminary statement the same question, and anyone else she ran into at the scene who looked as if they were law enforcement. She called it out across the lawn to Alvarez, who sent another uniformed officer to speak with her. "The detective says you should go home. They'll need a more complete statement. He'll call you and arrange it tomorrow."

But Alvarez had known she couldn't wait until the next day, and tired as he must have been, he had come to see her.

In the meantime, Jane had called Andy to tell him Megan was found. They'd both cried. She'd spoken to Harry, too, and he'd come to sit with her. He was concerned about her welfare, both physical and emotional, and fussed—Do you want tea? A bath? A glass of wine?—until she demanded he stop. The satellite trucks were back next door, broadcasting from the lawn. By the time Alvarez arrived, Jane and Harry were in the living room, the TV off, no music or other distractions, not talking, just sitting. Harry let Alvarez in, excused himself, and went into the kitchen.

Alvarez sat on the end of the couch nearest Jane's pink chair. "How are you?"

"Sore. But otherwise fine."

"That's a pretty scary thing he did to you."

"I don't think it's hit me yet. I'm more concerned about Megan. Is she okay?"

"She's dehydrated and weak. The hospital is going to keep her at least overnight."

"Was she able to tell you what happened?"

"Barely. She was awakened in the night by a noise. She thought someone was trying to break in. She tried to call 911 and ran for the panic room. That's the last thing she remembers until she woke up tied up in the back of Vreeland's van."

"Was she in her house the whole time?" Somehow it seemed worse if Megan was next door all along.

"She lost track of the days, and Vreeland isn't talking, but yes, it seems as if she was over there pretty much as soon as we finished with the scene and after you found the slipper in the panic room. Vreeland probably figured it was safe because we'd already searched it."

"And before that?"

"Before that she only remembers being in the back of his van."

It took Jane a moment to realize what that meant. "So she was there in the van, in the driveway, the day I found the panic room?"

"We were all there that day. She was bound and gagged, unable to move or cry out, so she couldn't attract our attention." He sounded as regretful as Jane felt.

"None of us thought to look in the windows of the van."

"Why would we have? *We* called *him* to the house."

They were silent for a moment. Jane imagined Alvarez was reexamining everything he had learned, thinking back over each step he'd taken. As she was. "Why did he do it?" she finally asked.

"I don't know. As I said, he's not talking, and we've just started looking at the computers and other stuff we took from his house and from Acme after his arrest. One thing is clear, she wasn't the only Acme client he watched."

"Were the others all attractive, single women?"

"No. That's the strange part. There was a family, an older

couple, three guy roommates from the other side of the city. He watched them all like he was watching a TV show. But over time, he watched Megan more. Obsessively."

"He must have known her father was gaslighting her."

"He must have known somebody was. Perhaps that's what drew his attention to her in particular."

"Of course it did. He was Justin the Guardian," Jane said. "You need to look more deeply into the lives of the other people he watched. They may also be under some kind of threat."

Alvarez grunted. "A threat from the outside or maybe even from inside the home. If he truly cares about the others in his twisted way, if he's Justin the Guardian, maybe he'll confess and tell us why he was watching so we can protect them now that he can't."

"The gaslighting and Megan's abduction were connected, but not in the way I assumed," Jane said. "I told her to turn the cameras off. That was the trigger. He couldn't watch her electronically, so he had to take her." She'd been thinking about it for a while, the timing of it all, the cause and the effect.

"We don't know that."

"You will. He'll confess, or it will be irrefutable when you look at what's on his computer. Soon you'll know." She couldn't hold back the tears that had formed in the corners of her eyes any longer. "I go around, thinking I'm helping, but I'm only blundering about. I've no more idea of what I'm doing than any other person. I'm a silly, old buttinski."

"Jane." Alvarez shocked her by taking her hand. "There is no possible way you could have anticipated that, in trying to help a young woman determine whether she was crazy, you would unleash a lunatic. And not even the one who was gaslighting her." He gave her hand a squeeze. "You are more than qualified to do what you do, and the world is a better place for it. Never underestimate the value of common sense."

Chapter Fifty-three

The next day Jane was sore, as predicted. She hobbled out of bed into a hot shower, gulped down ibuprofen, and determinedly got dressed. By the time she got downstairs, coffee was brewed, omelets were made, and there was a red rose beside her plate that almost made her weep. Harry left after a long (gentle) embrace, and Jane set off (slowly) down Old Deer Path.

Both of the Pilchners were home, which was lucky, though Ralph had to call Ceil twice before she came downstairs. Their living room was less chaotic than on Jane's previous visit. A row of plastic bins had been lined up under the living room windows to hold the toys. An accommodation to and acceptance of new life circumstances? Jane hoped so. The idea was central to what she planned to propose.

"I've thought about this a great deal," Jane said when

they were all seated. "Roo is, of course, your cat and you're entitled to have her live with you. She'll likely have to be an indoor cat, at least for the foreseeable future, to keep her from going over to the Marshalls' house."

"If they didn't let her in—" Ceil started.

"I'd like to suggest an alternative." Jane shifted in the chair, uncertain about how her message would be received. "Your lives have changed a great deal since Roo came to live with you. There are four additional people in the house, three of them children, and a dog and another cat."

"But—" Ceil protested. Ralph listened without comment.

"I think you're not unhappy with this new life. It's busy and you have the satisfaction of knowing you're supporting your son and grandchildren."

"Of course," Ceil said. "Of course we want to help out. And it is lovely having children in the house again, though it's also noisy and exhausting."

"And not what you expected at this point in your lives," Jane added.

"No, indeed," Ralph agreed.

"You chose this," Jane said. "You chose to welcome your son and his family even knowing the sacrifice. Roo didn't choose it. It's something that happened to her." Jane leaned forward to emphasize her words. "Roo prefers a quieter life. She's happy at the Marshalls', and they're happy to have her. You should let her stay with them."

They were silent for a moment. "I don't want to give her up," Ceil mumbled.

"I understand," Jane reassured her. "But embracing a

new way of life means giving up an old vision of how our lives will be. It's hard to let go, but it's necessary to do so to live in and enjoy a new reality."

"I see what you mean," Ceil admitted after a moment. "I only want what's best for Roo."

"You want what's best for everyone," Jane said. "Because you're good people."

Ralph walked Jane to the door, where he gave her a hug. "Thank you for this," he said. "I think it's all worked out for the best."

"Good-bye, Ralph. Good luck with the family."

Back home, Jane took a box of trash bags up to her room. She cleared out three drawers, two shelves, and a foot of hanger space. Then the soreness caught up with her. She took more ibuprofen and retired to her chair with a good book, waiting for Harry to return so she could tell him what she had done and they could move on to the next chapter in their lives.

Chapter Fifty-four

The cards were dealt. The bridge table was set up in Jane's living room, the game about to begin. It was a gray November day. Outside the wind pushed desiccated leaves across the sidewalk and swung the FOR SALE sign in front of Megan's house like a pendulum.

Helen turned from looking out the window. "I'm sorry she's gone."

"Honestly," Irma asked, "could you stay in a house after you'd been held prisoner there?"

"No." Helen shook her head. "I guess I couldn't."

"Still, she's given it all up. Her career, her friends. I hear she's gone off to somewhere in the Caribbean," Phyllis said.

"She'll have to come back for the trial," Helen pointed out.

"For both trials," Jane said. "Assuming neither Justin Vreeland nor her father reach a plea deal."

"No wonder she's fallen apart," Phyllis said. "Poor thing."

It was awful to be victimized as Megan had been. Financially and psychologically by a parent who should have loved and protected her, and physically and emotionally by a stranger. Most people would have been curled up in a corner.

Jane didn't believe Megan had fallen apart. The last time she'd seen her, Megan had been propped up on the couch in Andy Bromfield's condo, where her mother and Andy fussed over her. There was no doubt Megan had been through an experience no human being should have to endure. When Jane was leaving, she'd leaned in to give Megan a hug good-bye.

"I'll never be able to thank you enough," Megan had whispered. "I'm going to be all right. I know what I have to do."

Megan must have been traumatized by her ordeal, certainly, but she'd not only survived but thrived through a terrible childhood with one evil and one dysfunctional parent. She might well triumph again.

Laura Reeve had taken to calling Jane a couple of times a month. Her ostensible reason was to report on the welfare of Wembly, who now lived with her in the Berkshires. But they always ended up talking about Megan. Laura and her daughter had stayed in close touch. Andy Bromfield had declined the partnership he'd been offered at Bookerman, Digby, and Eade, the partnership that could have been Megan's. He'd sold his condo and moved what few sticks of furniture and personal items he'd kept into storage. He was in the Caribbean, too, traveling with Megan.

Jane remembered Megan's vision board. Tropical places, cats, and babies. Not one image of a fancy law office, a beautiful renovated home, a woman in a smart business outfit. Jane fervently hoped that Megan's trauma had propelled her not only away from something but toward something—the life she had wanted all along.

Acknowledgments

I hope you have enjoyed reading this tale of Jane Darrowfield's adventures as much as I have enjoyed writing it.

I would like to thank Tom Fritz, whose friendship goes back to our misspent high school days, for first mentioning digital gaslighting to me. The horrifying possibilities instantly made perfect sense to me because my husband and I have an alarm system at our house that he understands intimately and I can barely turn on and off. It's a good thing I don't have anyone with ill intent in my life.

I also thank Marty Jenkins, whose friendship goes back to our misspent college days, for reminding me about the finer points of bidding bridge hands. All mistakes are my own.

Thanks to my nephew Hume Ross for coaching me through the process of selecting equity partners in a large law firm. The process seems largely unchanged from when I worked in a fancy Boston law firm forty years ago. But I was a mere paralegal and not privy to the inner workings.

Thank you to Jessica Ellicott, who spent two lo-o-ong sessions with me talking about the possibilities for this book and whose enthusiasm for the story carried me along. Also, thanks to Sherry Harris, who read the manuscript and made amazing suggestions that made it so much stronger even while she was on a deadline of her own for the ninth Sarah Winston Garage Sale Mystery, *Absence of Alice*. As always, a shout-out to all my Wicked Authors, Jessica and Sherry, along with Julia Henry, Maddie Day, and Cate Conte.

Thank you to the entire team at Kensington, always professional, always inspired. I'd especially like to acknowledge my editor, John Scognamiglio, and my publicist, Larissa Ackerman. Thanks also to my agent, John Talbot.

Finally, thank you to my family. My wonderful husband, Bill Carito; my son and his family, Rob, Sunny, and Viola Carito; and my daughter and her family, Kate, Luke, Etta, and Sylvie Donius. I could not do it without your love and support.

Connect with U(s)

Visit us online at
KensingtonBooks.com
to read more from your favorite authors, see books
by series, view reading group guides, and more.

Join us on social media

for sneak peeks, chances to win books and prize packs,
and to share your thoughts with other readers.

facebook.com/kensingtonpublishing
twitter.com/kensingtonbooks

Tell us what you think!

To share your thoughts, submit a review,
or sign up for our eNewsletters, please visit:
KensingtonBooks.com/TellUs.